THE MAGNIFICENT LIZZIE BROWN AND THE GHOST SHIP

BY VICKI LOCKWOOD

COVER ILLUSTRATION BY STEPHANIE HANS

CAPSTONE YOUNG READERS
a capstone imprint

The Magnificent Lizzie Brown is published in the United States in 2016
by Capstone Young Readers,
A Capstone Imprint
1710 Roe Crest Drive
North Mankato, Minnesota 56003
www.capstoneyoungreaders.com

First published in 2015 by Curious Fox,
an imprint of Capstone Global Library Limited,
7 Pilgrim Street, London, EC4V 6LB
Registered company number: 6695582
www.curious-fox.com

Text © Hothouse Fiction Ltd 2015
Series created by Hothouse Fiction
www.hothousefiction.com

Library of Congress Cataloging-in-Publication Data can be found on the Library of Congress
website.

Summary: The adventures of the Magnificent Lizzie Brown continue as the traveling circus
heads to the English coast, invited by the mysterious Maharaja Duleep Singh. But something's
amiss at the small seaside town — fishermen claim a ghost ship haunts the harbor. And soon
after they arrive, Lizzie has a vision of a theft. Sure enough, a valuable necklace goes missing,
and several of Lizzie's friends are among the suspects. It's up to Lizzie and her friends to find
the thief and uncover the hidden secrets of the coastal town.

ISBN 978-1-4342-9806-5 (library binding) -- ISBN 978-1-62370-209-0 (paper over board) -- ISBN
978-1-4965-0215-5 (eBook PDF) -- ISBN 978-1-62370-583-1 (reflowable epub)

Designer: Kristi Carlson

Printed in China.
042015   008867RRDF15

For Laurie, the goblin market girl

With special thanks to
Adrian Bott

CHAPTER 1

Fitzy, who was both owner and ringmaster of the circus that bore his name, stood alone in the sawdust ring and lifted his gigantic hat to the audience in Oxford, England.

"Ladies and gentlemen of Oxford!" he shouted. "Dear friends, all of you! It has been a pleasure to entertain you for so many nights. But alas, all good things must come to an end."

The audience sighed an *awwww*, but Fitzy dismissed it. "No tears, I beg you. I ask only this — one final time, please show your appreciation for the stars of our show, every one of them!" He brandished his cane. "Maestro, please!"

As the band struck up a cheery tune, the various acts came prancing back into the massive show ring. The colored lights brightened, the audience cheered and clapped, and Fitzy stood among it all beaming like a lighthouse.

Nobody in the audience could see the two children who hid behind the beaded curtain, waving and grinning to their performer friends as they headed back out for a last hurrah. One was Lizzie Brown, the circus's resident fortune-teller, who — unlike most sideshow psychics — genuinely had the ability to see into the future. The other was Fitzy's son, Malachy, whose clubfoot couldn't slow down his razor-sharp mind.

"The Amazing Sullivan Sisters!" Fitzy announced.

Lizzie's best friends, the twins Erin and Nora, trotted past her on the backs of their flawless black horses, Victoria and Albert, named after the English queen and her husband. Both girls had long red hair plaited into braids fastened with silver barrettes, and they wore ballet dresses designed to be worn in the saddle.

Nora gave Lizzie a wave and wink. As they entered the ring, the twins stood up on their saddles, then tumbled over to do handstands. Lizzie watched, holding her breath with excitement, while the two girls entranced the audience once again.

Beside her, Malachy laughed. "It's the same show they do every night. Aren't you tired of watching yet?"

"Never," Lizzie said, shaking her head. How could she ever get tired of this? She was still new to the circus, true, but she knew the wonder of it all would never fade, no matter how much hard work needed to be done or how many early mornings had to be endured. This brightly colored world, always on the move, was where she belonged.

"Those merry masters of mayhem, the clowns!" Fitzy's voice rang out.

The clowns came charging past her in answer to Fitzy's call, but the moment they burst into the ring, they fell over, tumbling head-over-heels or slamming into one another. The audience roared with laughter, and Lizzie smiled to see her friend JoJo throwing buckets of confetti all around. Not long ago, he had been very sick with smallpox. Lizzie was happy to see that he was feeling better and back to his old self.

"Good crowd tonight," Malachy commented. "Best show in a long time."

"I bet your dad is pleased."

"Definitely. After Kensal Green, this is just what he needed. He looks ten years younger, doesn't he?"

Lizzie shuddered at the memory of Kensal Green. Setting up the circus so close to the biggest cemetery in London hadn't worked out very well. All the animals had been skittish, and the crowds were slow to come. Then Erin had been hurt too badly to perform, which meant no star performer and angry customers demanding refunds. On top of all that, there had been the strange affair of the Devil's Hound. Everything had worked out in the end, thanks to Lizzie and her friends, but it had nearly bankrupted Fitzy.

"Thank heaven nothing's gone wrong here in Oxford," Lizzie muttered. "Not so far, anyway."

She hadn't said anything to Malachy, but that was her other reason for watching the show every night. It was becoming a superstition. She didn't dare miss it, in case something bad happened.

"The Astonishing Boissets!" Fitzy announced, hurling his cane up into the air.

The lights swiveled to reveal the high wire. The audience gasped as the family of French daredevils came out onto it to take their bows. The wire trembled under their weight. Dru Boisset was in the center — dark-haired, handsome, and all of fourteen years old.

Lizzie's knuckles went to her mouth. No matter how many times she saw their act, her stomach was always in knots. Even the presence of the safety net didn't help.

Malachy grinned. "Do you think he can see you from up there?"

"What?" Lizzie glared at him.

"Does he know you watch him every night? Don't worry. I won't tell. But we both know why you're really here, Lizzie."

"You brat!" Lizzie cried, storming toward him with her fist raised.

Malachy cringed away, laughing.

"Dru's just a friend, and you know it," Lizzie insisted. "But I've seen *you* making puppy dog eyes at the twins!" *Sooner or later*, she thought, *I'll figure out which one Mal has a crush on.*

8

Mal rolled his eyes. "Whatever you say."

"One of these days I'll give you a fat lip," Lizzie grumbled. She wasn't really angry, and Malachy was hardly the only one of her friends who teased her about Dru. But if she didn't lash out like this, they might realize that the sight of the boy really *did* make her heart go all fluttery.

Fitzy introduced the tumbling acrobats, then the boys of the Sullivan family riding their ponies, and finally the stately elephants led by Hari, the Indian boy who was another of Lizzie's close friends.

Lizzie was was determined not to stare at Dru now, just to prove Malachy wrong, so she let her gaze rove over the audience instead. They really were an impressive bunch, this Oxford crowd. Men with top hats like a row of chimneys, ladies with skin as pale as bone china, children in sailor suits bouncing up and down in their seats. Lizzie guessed not one of those rosy-faced kids knew what it was like to go without a single meal, let alone face starvation.

Back in the days when she'd lived in the London slum of Rat's Castle, Lizzie would have been jealous of children like that. They had lollipops and toys, while she had to struggle for a crust of bread. But her fortune-telling had taught her some surprising lessons — even the richest of families could have terrible secrets, she now knew, and a pampered childhood didn't always mean happiness.

"Thank you once again, ladies and gentlemen, and good night!" Fitzy called out in the ring.

As he bowed, turned, and bowed again, Lizzie noticed something strange in the front row. In the row of top hats, one of the heads was covered in bandages. No, not bandages — a turban!

Lizzie could see the gentleman clearly now. "Whoa," she said, impressed. He was strikingly handsome, with dark skin like Hari's and elegantly cut clothes. Definitely not lacking in money, then. And were those jeweled rings on his fingers?

The English people beside him were clapping politely, but the stylish gentleman was showing no such restraint. *"Bravo!"* he shouted, applauding wildly. *"Encore!"*

Lizzie grinned to see an adult enjoying himself so much. Usually, only children would react with this kind of wild excitement. Either this man didn't realize it was considered improper to go overboard like this, or he didn't care. Nobody was shushing him, at any rate. Maybe they didn't dare to.

The lady sitting next to him was smiling and looking at him fondly. She was blond and beautiful, like a painting from the top of a box of chocolates.

Is that his wife? Lizzie wondered. The woman looked familiar and she was sure she must have seen her somewhere before, in the papers, maybe. She looked like a society lady or perhaps an actress or a foreign princess. The woman was slowly fanning herself with a broad fan made of peacock feathers, and Lizzie was reminded of the way a cat's tail would sometimes swish back and forth slowly as it sat thinking.

All at once *the feeling* was upon her, gripping Lizzie's whole body as suddenly as a sneeze and every bit as impossible to control. She let out a tiny gasp, and then stood still as the pictures began to appear in her mind.

I'm having one of my visions! she thought, fearful and excited at once. Most of the time, Lizzie's visions appeared when she was doing readings for people, but they sometimes struck out of the blue, just like this one. The unexpected visions were much stronger than the others, and they always warned of trouble to come . . .

She saw herself outside, at night, somewhere cold. She was standing in a curved archway. Reaching out to touch the sides of the arch, she realized that it was made of bone.

Moving in slow motion, Lizzie passed through the archway and found herself overlooking the vast sea. She was standing at the top of a rocky cliff, breathing the salt air and hearing the cries of the gulls. There was something haunted about this strange place.

Far below she saw a tidy seaside village. There were buildings clustered on the sides of a dip in the land, a ruin on a cliff . . . and out at sea, but drawing closer, a ship surrounded by mist like something out of a ghost story. A strange green light shone from it . . .

Someone was poking her hard in the arm — Malachy. "You all right?" he asked, sounding doubtful.

Lizzie blinked, coming back to herself, then shuddered and blew air out — *phew!* "I had a vision. It wasn't a blurry one, so I know it wasn't the past. It was clear, so it must have been showing me the future."

"Was there a crime going on?" Malachy suddenly sounded excited, and with good reason. Lizzie's visions had predicted crimes in the past, crimes that their circle of friends — the Penny Gaff Gang, as they had named themselves, after the popular theater performances known as "penny gaffs" — had managed to stop.

"No," said Lizzie, puzzled. "I was at the seaside. At least I think I was."

"Huh?"

Lizzie shook her head. "I've never even seen the sea before. But there was so much water, it had to be the sea. And a town, and bones, and this weird ship in a cloud of mist."

"The seaside." Malachy laughed. "I reckon you're losing your touch, mate. We're off to Reading next. There're no beaches there! No jellied eels, neither!"

"Reading?" Lizzie repeated. "But it was so clear!" She frowned. She'd never considered what would happen if her powers abandoned her, or worse, led her in the wrong direction. She'd just be a crazy girl then, fit only for a mental hospital.

* * *

After the show, the circus people all packed into the tea tent for the traditional last night party. There was wine for the adults, lemonade for the kids, and cake for everyone. Lizzie grinned to see Rice Pudding Pete, the messiest of the clowns, nibble daintily at his cake as if he were a society lady.

"Where's Fitzy?" asked Nora through a mouthful of crumbs.

"He went off to talk in private," Ma Sullivan told her with a knowing look.

"With who?"

"A person with a big bank account. That's all I'm saying."

Lizzie was certain she knew who Fitzy was talking to. "It was that man with the turban, wasn't it?"

Ma Sullivan gave her a quelling look. "I reckon you'll all find out soon enough."

As it turned out, they only had to wait a few seconds. Fitzy strolled into the tea tent with the turbaned gentleman by his side, beaming at the crowd.

"If I could have your attention for a moment?" Fitzy called. "This, my friends, is Maharaja Gurinder Bhatti."

Lizzie and Nora looked at one another, open-mouthed. "A maharaja? I think that's like a king or something!" whispered Lizzie.

"It is a pleasure to meet you all," the Maharaja said with just a hint of an Indian accent. "May I?" He helped

13

himself to a piece of cake and made a face as if he'd just tasted heaven. "Mmm. This is wonderful."

Ma Sullivan giggled like a schoolgirl and seemed suddenly unable to speak a word.

"The Maharaja has told me how much he enjoyed our little show tonight," Fitzy continued. "I am delighted to tell you that we've been invited to put on a special performance —"

"Please be my guests in Whitby," the Maharaja interrupted eagerly. "I've just rented Dunsley Castle, and I think my new neighbors in the town would love a circus."

"Naturally, I have accepted. We can hardly refuse a royal command!" Fitzy told the stunned crowd.

"Please," the Maharaja said, "it is a request, no more."

"Your Majesty, your merest request is our command," Fitzy insisted. "Next weekend, we shall be in Whitby to entertain the locals. Now, Maharaja, a glass of champagne?"

As the drinks were poured, everyone broke into excited conversation.

"Where's Whitby?" Lizzie asked Malachy.

Malachy said nothing.

"Why are you looking at me like that?"

"Whitby's in North Yorkshire. It's a seaside town." Malachy sighed. "I know, I know. We're going to the seaside after all. You saw it coming. When will I learn? Your visions are never wrong, are they?"

"Not so far," Lizzie laughed, relieved.

Anita, billed as the World's Smallest Woman, seemed less thrilled than everyone else. "It's very kind of the Maharaja, I'm sure, but it will take us forever to get up to Whitby. Plodding along in our old horse-drawn carriages, we'll be on the road for a week!"

"I think you may find it takes a lot less time than that," Fitzy said.

Anita folded her arms and snorted. "Oh? What do you have in mind, Fitzy? A flying carpet?"

But Fitzy's only answer was a secretive smile.

CHAPTER 2

Lizzie stood on the train platform and swallowed nervously. The train loomed before her, a mechanical beast, its smoke stack belching, and its pistons like metal bones. Steam hissed around Lizzie's ankles like dragon breath. Now that she actually had to get *on* it, the prospect of her first-ever train journey was more terrifying than exciting.

"Come on, Lizzie!" Nora and Erin called together, sticking their heads out of the train window.

"If you don't get on the train, you'll have to walk," Nora shouted.

"And it's a long way to Whitby!" added Erin.

All around Lizzie, the circus people were climbing on board, chatting excitedly and hauling bulging bags. Many of them were waving out of the windows, shouting to late arrivals to hurry up.

Lizzie just stood as if she'd been turned to stone. She stared at the gap between the station platform and the train car. *People must fall down there all the time,* she

16

imagined. *They must get sliced to pieces by those huge iron wheels.*

Malachy was already on board as well. "The Maharaja has rented a whole train, just for us! Isn't it amazing?" he'd said to her before aggressively barging past everyone else to be one of the first on board.

Well, Lizzie didn't think it was amazing. It was a monstrous thing, this locomotive, hissing and clanking and stinking of scorched metal, like an iron left too long in the fire.

"They explode," Lizzie muttered to herself. "I've read it in the papers. The boilers go bang. Terrible tragedy. Hundreds dead."

"Lizzie, come *on!*" Nora beckoned. "You'll miss it!"

"I'll just be a minute," Lizzie shouted. She took a deep breath, counted to three, and took a single bold step toward the train.

At that moment, the whistle screeched and the smoke stack let out a belch of white steam. Lizzie immediately squealed in horror and scrambled back away from it. She sat down on a bench, panting heavily.

Just then Dru sauntered past, wearing a dress coat and looking every inch the young gentleman. He either hadn't seen her or was pretending he hadn't, but either way he suddenly stopped in his tracks and turned to her with a smile. "Ah, Lizzie. This is your first time on a train, *n'est-ce pas?*"

"It will be, if I ever get on the darn thing," she muttered.

Dru crossed the platform, stepped onto the train, and held out his hand. "Come, *ma chère amie*. Do not worry. I will protect you."

Without a second thought, Lizzie stormed toward him. She ignored his hand and left it hanging in the air as she stepped up, pushed past him, and threw herself into the train car. She flopped down into the nearest seat, alongside Nora and Erin, who squealed with glee.

Dru followed her into the car and raised an eyebrow at Lizzie. "Girls," he said with a shrug. "Always contradictory."

"It's only a train," Lizzie scoffed as if her heart wasn't hammering in her chest. She smoothed down her skirt and crossed her legs. Then she uncrossed them and set her bag on her lap. How were you supposed to sit in a train car, anyway?

A station guard waved a flag and blew a quick *peep-peep* on his whistle. Erin grinned at her. "We'll start moving any minute!"

"We'll be in Yorkshire tomorrow morning, just one day after leaving Oxford!" Nora exclaimed. "I can't believe it. It's magic. Like something out of *Tales of the Arabian Nights*."

"The Maharaja isn't Arabian," Dru told her. "He's Indian."

"He's rich is what he is!" said Erin, laughing. "And he knows exactly what to do with his money. When I'm rich, I'm going to rent whole trains for my friends to ride around in, too."

The train lurched forward.

"Oh, god!" Lizzie gasped, frantically grabbing her seat. "Oh, no. Make it stop. I need to get off."

"Don't be silly, Lizzie," said Nora. "Relax. Enjoy the ride."

"Enjoy the ride?" Lizzie repeated as if Nora had told her to eat a tasty frog. "You're crazy. Oh no, we're going even faster!"

"We haven't even left the station yet, Lizzie," Dru pointed out.

Lizzie covered her face and moaned. She stayed that way for a whole minute. Then she asked, "Are we in Yorkshire yet?"

"Lizzie, seriously now, calm down," Nora said, putting an arm around Lizzie's shoulders. "We'll be on this train for a few hours to come, so you'd better get used to it and stop acting like such a fool."

Lizzie slowly lowered her hands and looked out the window, catching a last glimpse of the train station. She desperately wished she was plodding along in her shabby wagon, which she'd taken to calling Old Esther. "It can't be safe," she whispered. "It just can't. God didn't mean for us to go this fast. It ain't natural."

Lizzie gripped her seat and stayed clamped there like a crab as the train chugged out of Oxford and picked up speed. Town buildings gave way to green fields and hedges as the countryside volleyed past. At first, she felt like she was trapped in a carriage pulled by runaway horses, but after a while, she started getting used to the sensation. Her fingers gradually relaxed their grip, her breathing slowed down, and her heart stopped trying to batter its way out of her ribcage.

Cows and sheep shot past the window. Not enough time to count them. From across the rattling, swaying train car, Dru gave her a smile.

Malachy and Hari appeared at the door to their compartment. "Guess who's been up front with the driver?" Malachy said proudly.

"Better you than me," Lizzie muttered.

Malachy, looking extremely proud, ignored her. "He reckons I'm a natural!"

"Just in time for a picnic, Mal, now that the gang's all here," Nora said. She and Erin unpacked a wicker basket, laying out sandwiches, an Irish potato dish called "colcannon" made with green onions and cream, and the remains of last night's cake.

"You all go ahead," Malachy told them. "I need to check Dad's accounts." He opened a fat ledger and ran his finger down the columns of figures, muttering sums to himself.

The rest of the Penny Gaff Gang eagerly dug into the food, and somewhere in the middle of her third slice of cake, Lizzie somehow forgot all about being scared of the train.

"Your mum makes the best cake in the world," she said, licking her fingers.

"This isn't even her best!" Erin said. "Just you wait until our birthday. The cake she makes then . . . oh, you'll die — of pure pleasure!"

"Just over a week to go!" Nora said, her voice rising to an excited squeak.

"It's the day after the big Whitby show," said Erin. "So don't go making any big plans, because there's going to be a party, and of course you're invited."

"When's your birthday?" Nora asked, turning to Lizzie. "We need to throw you a party."

"Maybe she doesn't like parties," Erin argued with her sister.

"Don't be silly. Everyone likes parties. Or maybe there's something you do instead? Something special?" Nora continued, still looking at Lizzie.

Erin looked closely at her friend. "What *do* you do on your birthday?"

"Don't do anything," Lizzie said with a sigh.

"What?" the twins said, horrified.

Lizzie shrugged. "Back in Rat's Castle, nobody cared about birthdays. They were just like any other day. I've

21

never even been to a birthday party, let alone had one of my own."

Erin and Nora looked shocked, then hugged her, one on each side. "We're going to do something about that," Nora said. "Aren't we, Erin?"

"That's right."

Lizzie gave the twins a grateful smile. The narrow streets and mean, grimy rooms of London's Rat's Castle slum were a long way away now. But sometimes, in her dreams, she would think she was back there. Pa would loom over her again, his breath stinking of beer and his rough fists brandished in her face. It had been a hungry, frightened life for a young girl, with no hope in sight.

Then salvation had come, parading through the streets in gold and glitter — Fitzy's Traveling Circus, filled with the most marvelous, unusual people Lizzie had ever known. Back then, people like the Amazon Queen and the World's Smallest Woman had been things of wonder to Lizzie. Now they were her friends.

I'll always be in Fitzy's debt, Lizzie thought to herself. *He took me on before I showed any sign of having psychic powers, just out of the goodness of his heart.*

Suddenly Fitzy was there in person, poking his head around their compartment door and grinning just like Malachy. "Everyone enjoying the ride?"

"It's fantastic!" Malachy yelled.

"Smashing!" said Nora and Erin together.

Dru shrugged and stretched his strong arms over his head. "It's a very relaxing way to travel, Fitzy. I might even take a *petit* nap."

"And you, Lizzie?"

Lizzie smiled weakly. "Didn't like it at first, but I'm getting used to it."

"We're on the road to riches, my young friends," Fitzy said, rubbing his hands together. "A royal command performance! Did you all know the Maharaja is one of Queen Victoria's favorites? Hopefully he'll tell all his rich friends about our circus." He rubbed the fabric of the seat cushions and smiled approvingly. "If the cash keeps coming in like this, we can buy a train of our own. A circus train. The first of its kind in the country."

Malachy looked up from the accounts ledger. "Don't get ahead of yourself, Dad."

"*Woo woo!*" cried Fitzy, tooting an imaginary train whistle. "Oh, Hari, I nearly forgot. Your uncle Zezete needs your help back in the animal car."

Hari leaped to his feet. "Are the animals okay?"

Fitzy nodded. "Oh, none of them are hurt. They're just not getting into the spirit of the train ride like you young people are."

"They're scared," Hari said, quickly swallowing his last bite of cake. "I'll be right there."

Lizzie felt a pang of sympathy. Poor animals — they didn't understand what was happening to them. They weren't used to the strange smells and horrible noises, or the rocking and swaying back and forth. She knew exactly how they felt.

"Hang on, Hari," Lizzie called after him. "I'm coming too."

* * *

When they arrived in the animals' car, Akula the elephant lay on her side in the straw. Her legs twitched and kicked erratically, like a dog dreaming of chasing rabbits. Her eyes were full of fear and her body trembled as if she were freezing cold.

"She's petrified!" Lizzie exclaimed. "We must help her!"

"Keep your voice down," Hari told her. She knew he wasn't angry; he was just letting her know how best to calm the elephant. Hari knelt down by Akula's huge head and stroked her trunk gently. "There now, pretty girl. Calm now. All's well."

"What can I do?"

"Stroke her ears, slowly. She likes that."

Together, the two friends worked to sooth Akula. Hari sang Indian songs, weaving melodies that sounded strange and beautiful to Lizzie. All the notes went up and down like fireflies dancing in the night sky. She didn't understand a word, of course, but the syllables were softly enchanting, with the dark beauty of peacock feathers and gleaming jewels.

When Zezete came in, bringing a bucket of feed, he said nothing at first. He simply squatted down and watched Hari and Lizzie at work together. When Akula fell into a happy sleep, he smiled.

"You have a real gift for working with the elephants, Lizzie," he said. "If you ever grow tired of being the circus's fortune-teller, you can always join us as an animal handler."

Lizzie just smiled. "I like the songs you were singing," she told Hari. "Are they from India?"

"No, Lizzie," Hari said, his face very serious. "They are from the moon."

Lizzie stared, then cracked up laughing. "Ask a silly question! So . . . do you two know anything about the Maharaja, then? He's Indian, isn't he? Fitzy says he's one of Queen Victoria's favorites!"

Zezete spat on the floor and muttered something harsh-sounding. He wasn't speaking English. Hari glanced nervously at his uncle, then looked down at the ground. Lizzie had the creeping feeling that she'd said something foolish.

"I need to feed the camels," Zezete said, in English this time. His voice was colder than Lizzie had ever heard it before. The next second, he was gone without a backward glance.

"Hari, I didn't mean —"

"I know," Hari interrupted. "And Zezete knows, too. He won't be angry with you. But you'd best let him cool down."

"What did I do?" Lizzie asked, confused.

Hari sighed. "It's a long story. Ugly, too. You're sure you want to hear it?"

"Yes!"

The two friends leaned against Akula's back as she slept, peacefully now, while Hari patiently explained what had made his uncle so angry.

"Gurinder Bhatti may be the latest society favorite here in England," he began, "but to us Indians, he's a traitor. He was a prince of Punjab, but he sold his country to the British East India Company."

Lizzie struggled to imagine selling a whole country to a foreign power.

"He gave England the Khyber Diamond, too," Hari continued, sounding almost as angry as Zezete had. "All that stuff your queen says about India being the jewel in her crown? That jewel's stolen property, and the likes of Gurinder Bhatti are responsible."

"But . . . he seemed so nice." Lizzie could hardly believe that the good-natured man had betrayed millions of Indians, all for money.

"Oh, he knows how to play the part of the dashing prince," Hari said sourly. "He's handsome and wealthy, and the toast of British high society and friends with Queen Victoria, but he's not exactly popular back home!"

CHAPTER 3

Lizzie woke up in darkness amid the smell of straw. She was still lying against Akula's warm, heaving flank. She must have dozed off, she realized. *Not the smartest thing in the world, falling asleep curled up with an elephant. What if she had rolled over in the night and flattened me?*

What a silly thought. Akula would never do that. Lizzie felt safe around the huge animal, even when she was asleep. She felt around until she found Akula's head, gave it a loving pat, then stood up and brushed the straw from her dress.

What time is it? Lizzie wondered. The train was still rattling along. She opened the door to the next car, letting in the gray light of morning, and groped her way blearily through the train until she found her own spot.

Her friends were all where she had left them, but now they were slumped snoring in their seats. Dru had propped his feet on the seats across from him, Malachy was using the ledger as a pillow, and Erin and Nora were clutching each other as if they feared being parted.

Lizzie stepped over Dru's legs. She watched him sleep for a moment, then felt funny about it and settled into her own empty seat by the window. Nobody woke up.

She didn't mind the speed of the train at all now. Odd how quickly you could get used to new things. Through the window, Lizzie watched the sun come up over wide, rolling countryside, much of it empty and rugged but beautiful. She saw dry stone walls, sheep nestled into the green grass, rocky rough slopes, and acres of desolate moorland — large areas of rolling, often wet, land full of plant life. The cottages were stony and small, like holdovers from some earlier part of history.

Malachy stirred and opened his eyes. "Morning," he mumbled. Yawning, he asked, "Where are we?"

"Somewhere with a lot of moors."

"We must be in North Yorkshire! Yes — see that river down there, all silvery and twisting like it was made of metal? That's the Esk River. It flows down to the sea at Whitby."

Lizzie clenched her hands together with excitement. "We're almost there!"

Her loud voice woke up the others. Sleepiness soon vanished like morning dew as they realized how close to Whitby they were. Suddenly, the last few miles of the journey seemed like the longest of all.

Lizzie couldn't stop staring at the river. It meant the seaside was close. Ever since she was little, she'd dreamed of going to the beach one day. The closest she'd ever come was the muddy banks of London's Thames River.

Out on the moors, people were leading ponies carrying heavy packs. "What are they doing up so early?" Lizzie wondered aloud. "They can't be farmers."

"They're probably bringing rough jet home from the coast," Malachy explained. "You know what jet is, don't you?"

"Something . . . black?" Lizzie guessed. "'Cause people say 'jet black,' don't they?"

Malachy nodded. "That's right. It's a shiny black stone. I bet that's what's in those packs. Huge lumps of rough jet."

"And the Whitby jewelers make it into brooches, bracelets, rings, and necklaces," Nora cut in. "It's beautiful stuff."

Malachy chuckled. "Funny to think of fine ladies wearing jewelry made from fossilized trees. That's what jet is, you know."

"Malachy!"

"Like wearing coal, really — ow! Nora, stop kicking me!"

* * *

The last leg of the journey was on the road. The brightly colored circus wagons were wheeled down from the train on ramps with loving care and reunited with their horses and ponies. They only had a few miles to travel, and Dunsley Castle was soon in view over the treetops.

"It's a real castle!" Lizzie gasped, standing up on the roof of her wagon. Her old home had been called "Rat's Castle" as a bitter joke. What would the people back there say if they could see her now?

"Fit for a princess!" Malachy called across.

"It's so funny, being here so suddenly," Lizzie said dreamily. "Seems like no time has passed at all. Like a giant scooped up the whole circus, wagons and all, and plonked us down here."

"Smell that salt air?" Hari took a deep breath. "You can tell we're close to the sea."

"I can't wait!" The palms of Lizzie's hands itched with anticipation.

"You're going to have to wait," Malachy reminded her. "We all are. Can't go running off until the tents are all pitched."

That brought her back down to earth with a bump. "Sometimes, Mal, you really remind me of your dad," she said.

But the truth was, Lizzie wasn't one to avoid hard work. From the moment the circus convoy pulled up on the gravel forecourt of Dunsley Castle, she threw herself into the work along with the rest of the company. For the next three hours, she helped to unroll huge sheets of canvas, haul bundles of poles in multiple sections, pound thick tent pegs into the ground, and unload endless boxes of props and costumes.

The grassy lawns were thick and lush, the finest she'd ever seen. The flowerbeds nearby were peppered with blooms. Bashing stakes into the ground felt a little bit like vandalism, but this was where the Maharaja wanted them to perform, so this was where the tents would be pitched.

After all, Lizzie thought, *it's his garden and he can do what he wants with it.*

She and Dru worked their way around the outside of a tent, Dru holding the stakes in place and Lizzie walloping them into the ground with a mallet. She couldn't take her eyes off the stunning castle behind them; with its parapets and towers, it looked like something straight out of medieval times.

In reality it wasn't that old — most of the really old castles were nothing but ruins now. And Dunsley Castle was really just a manor house, made to look like a castle. Even so, Lizzie could imagine princesses walking along the balconies, their long silken dresses fluttering in a warm summer's breeze . . .

Lost in her dreams, she swung and missed the stake completely. The mallet whacked into the grass, gouging out a chunk of earth. Dru sprang away with an acrobat's reflexes.

"Lizzie, watch what you're doing *s'il vous plaît!*"

"Sorry!" Lizzie folded her arms and leaned on the mallet handle. "It's just that I think I've fallen in love with that house."

"An Englishman's home is his castle," Dru teased. "Maybe an English*woman's*, too."

Lizzie just snorted at that. She lifted the mallet, and Dru went back to work with a merry whistle.

By mid-afternoon, the red-and-white striped show tent was in place, towering over all the smaller tents. To one side, a staked-out corral enclosed the circus ponies, who were happily munching the lush grass. Lizzie was glad to see they seemed none the worse after their long journey on the train. Erin, Nora, and the other Sullivan siblings — Patrick and Sean, Brendan and Conor — sat on the grass beside them on a blanket, enjoying yet another picnic.

As Lizzie bashed in the last of the pegs, a furious yell resounded from the castle. "Hey!" came the shout, and then again, *"Hey!"*

Dru looked up, puzzled. "The Maharaja?"

Lizzie shook her head. "Didn't sound like him."

It wasn't. The man running toward them was white, hefty, and wore moleskin pants with suspenders, a scarf, and a cap. His whiskers were graying, and a huge wart protruded from the side of his nose. He carried a shovel over his shoulder like a musket.

He looks like a sprouting potato, thought Lizzie, *lumpy and grubby*.

The man glared at Lizzie as he passed, then continued until he reached the Sullivans. "What the 'ell do you mean by letting your animals rove on this 'ere grass?" Based on his accent, Lizzie figured out that he had to be a local man. "Are you aware you're trespassin' on private property?"

Nora burst out, "We was only —"

"Irish, is it?" The man scoffed. "We don't want no gypsy freeloaders round 'ere. You'd better move on before I start movin' yer."

To prove he meant it, the man held the shovel like a club, menacing Sean with it, and Lizzie felt a cold fear that the young man would jump to his feet and knock the older man out cold. His sisters were being threatened, and Sean never allowed that.

But to Lizzie's relief, Sean kept his cool. "I don't believe we've been introduced," he said with smooth good manners. "We're the Sullivans. It's a pleasure to meet you. And you are?"

"My name's Johnson, you fool!" roared the man. Lizzie couldn't tell whether it was Sean's cocky attitude that had set him off or his refusal to be intimidated. "These are my gardens your horses are chewing up!"

"Aren't they the Maharaja's gardens?" Erin asked, taking her cue from Sean and acting unruffled. "Ham sandwich, Mr. Johnson?"

"You can stuff your stupid sandwiches," Johnson yelled, purple in the face now.

More like a beet than a potato, Lizzie thought. He lurched forward as if he really meant to hit someone with his shovel.

Hari came running over. "What's the matter? Why all the shouting?"

Johnson rolled his eyes at the sight of Hari. "That's all we need. Another one."

"Another what?"

Johnson didn't answer the question. "I'm the gardener here at Dunsley Castle, I'll have you know. Do you have any idea how much work it takes to keep these gardens immaculate? And here you lot come, loosing horses on 'em, banging stakes in, heaven knows what else!" A sneer came over his face. "You've probably got elephants in them tents, haven't you?"

"Two, actually," Hari said. His white teeth gleamed as he smiled broadly. "I'm very proud of them."

When he realized that Hari was serious, Johnson's face went through several amazing contortions. He looked as though he was having a heart attack.

"We have every right to be here, Mr. Johnson," Hari said politely. "We're invited guests of the Maharaja. We're not squatters."

Johnson's voice went very quiet at that. "You don't belong here," he hissed. "Mark my words. When it all blows up in your faces — and it will — don't say I didn't warn you."

"This is gettin' out of hand," Lizzie told Dru. "Let's get Fitzy before someone gets hurt."

Thankfully the ringmaster was already hurrying over, with Malachy close behind. "Mr. Johnson, I'm so sorry. You should have been notified of our arrival. The message must have gone astray."

"You've turned these grounds into a farmyard," Johnson raged at him. "This place has been tended for hundreds of years, and you come rolling in and treat it like a public park! I'll be making a formal complaint about this."

"I promise you, on my word of honor, that we'll be respectful of the grounds." Fitzy's voice had a calm authority that even the gardener couldn't deny. All his ranting and bluster suddenly looked ridiculous next to Fitzy's well-mannered goodwill, and he fidgeted like a schoolboy caught throwing paper airplanes.

Lizzie was quietly impressed. Fitzy was surely as exhausted as everyone else, but he was still the solid rock on which the whole circus rested.

Johnson shrank into himself like a toad. He glanced around the lawn, finally letting his gaze rest on Hari. "You people . . ." he muttered, adding something Lizzie couldn't hear, but that sounded obscene. "Him, too. He'll be sorry. There's an evil wind coming, you mark me. And when the devil sails into Whitby harbor on his ghost ship, he'll find no shortage of sinners to carry off!"

With that, the gardener stomped off toward the castle, lifting his legs high with each step as if he·were wading through mud.

"Ghost ship?" said Nora, looking worried.

"He's just trying to scare us with superstitious nonsense," Lizzie said firmly. But in the back of her mind, she remembered the ghostly green ship she'd seen in her vision. *Could the groundskeeper be right?* she wondered. Had she foreseen the devil sailing into Whitby harbor?

"What an unpleasant little man," Fitzy said, holding his chin thoughtfully. Then he shrugged, as if the matter was already forgotten. "Let's move the horses around, folks. Not too much grazing in any one place, okay?"

"Right," Erin said with a salute.

Fitzy headed off to inspect the big top, while Malachy lingered to help finish off the picnic. Lizzie was still watching Johnson dwindle into the distance, leaving a trail of swear words hanging on the air.

"What's the matter with him, anyway?" she wondered aloud. "The Maharaja's giving the locals a circus for free, isn't he? You'd think he'd be happy, not acting like . . . like an angry badger!"

"Think about it, Liz," Malachy said, digging the last of the jam out of the jar with a finger. "The locals probably didn't like the Maharaja from the start. That's the real reason he's giving them a circus. To try and win them over."

"But . . . he's rich, he's popular, why would the people here hate him?" Lizzie asked.

Malachy and Hari exchanged a glance.

"Oh," Lizzie said. "It's because he's foreign, isn't it?"

"Foreign and brown-skinned," Hari said in a voice that hurt Lizzie's heart. "You heard what he said to me. 'Another one.' I'm not even from the Punjab. I'm from Goa."

"Not every community opens its arms as readily as Fitzy's circus," Malachy said sadly. "Some people just hate anyone who's different from them."

Lizzie thought how much wealth the Maharaja would bring to this town. "Even if they have lots of money?"

Malachy looked sour. "Especially if they have lots of money. It's even easier to hate someone you're jealous of."

CHAPTER 4

"Come in," said Fitzy, in answer to the knock on his wagon door.

"The tents are all up," Lizzie said breathlessly. The rest of the Penny Gaff Gang waited behind her, as eager as she was. "Hari's seen to the animals, and everyone's settled in all right, so . . ."

"Hmm," Fitzy said, turning to face her. "And I suppose you all want to go off into town now that all the hard work's done, do you?"

"Please," Lizzie said, biting her lip.

Fitzy gave her a hard stare, then broke into a wide grin. "Of course you can. Off you go." They were already sprinting away when he added, "Enjoy yourselves. *But —*"

Fitzy's last word stopped them all in their tracks, like dogs suddenly coming to the ends of their leashes. Lizzie, yearning to leave, turned to see what more he could possibly want.

Fitzy passed her a thick stack of fliers and a jar of paste. "Make yourselves useful while you're there," he said. "I want posters up wherever there's empty space, you understand? Be polite, it costs nothing. Ask in the shops if they'll stick one up in the window or by the door. But none on any private property without the owner's permission, and for heaven's sake don't stick 'em on any churches or memorials or things like that. We've already had one angry local giving us a piece of his mind."

"He had very few pieces left to give, if you ask me," Malachy muttered, making the others laugh.

Fitzy smiled too, despite himself. "Just remember your manners, understood?"

"What about selling tickets?" Lizzie asked. It was part of the usual routine when they arrived in a new town, and she was good at it.

Fitzy knocked gently on the top of her head with his knuckles, as if he were expecting a hollow sound. "It's a free show, remember? Our good friend the Maharaja's footing the bill."

Lizzie rolled her eyes, feeling silly for having forgotten. Then she took off after the others, who were already running across the grass.

"Careful of the lawn!" Fitzy bellowed. "And be back here by six or there'll be hell to pay!"

* * *

The walk back into Whitby led along a coastal road. Lizzie's first sight of the sea, so huge and broad and glittering, made her stomach clench with nervous excitement. "It's the sea," she whispered to herself. "It's really the sea . . ."

"Blimey," said Malachy, "so it is."

The sight of the light dancing on the water was a beautiful agony to Lizzie. The sea had woken a strange, deep, aching hunger in her. She feared it, and yet she craved it at the same time. Back in Kensal Green, she'd nearly drowned in the Grand Union canal. People from Rat's Castle rarely learned how to swim unless they were sailors. Since then, she'd been wary of the water.

"We should make a plan," Malachy said. "Figure out who wants to do what."

"Look in the shops," said Erin and Nora together.

"Hunt for fossils on the beach," said Hari.

Dru just shrugged. "I don't mind. Whatever the girls want to do."

"And you, Lizzie?"

"I want to sit on the beach," she said firmly. She could always watch the sea from a safe spot and maybe paddle in it if she felt brave enough.

"Okay, then." Malachy began a determined stride forward. "We'd better get going."

The town of Whitby lay on sloping land that ran down to the river. The roads wove back and forth, sometimes doubling back on each other like a mountain pass, sometimes driving steeply downhill toward the water. The buildings were all at different heights, lying at different levels on the slopes. From a distance, it looked as if you could jump from the higher roofs to the lower ones.

Lizzie spotted the whalebone arch from her vision at the top of the west cliff. On the opposite side of the bay, high on the eastern cliff, was the stone ruin she'd seen. That, she now knew, was Whitby Abbey. Even in this bright daylight, it seemed lonely and faintly sinister. There was no sign of the strange fog-shrouded ship.

Suddenly, Johnson's words came back to her. *"When the devil sails into Whitby harbor . . ."* And just like that, Lizzie knew with a cold certainty that there was a mystery here, something dark and unspoken that hovered over the town like a mist.

* * *

Lizzie badly wanted to run down the steep steps to the beach, but she knew they had work to do first. There were posters to put up and goodwill to spread. They strolled along the main shopping street, putting up posters wherever they could.

The jewelry store on the main street was called Delingpole's. The windows were stocked with sparkling jet, as black and shiny as molasses. Lizzie hadn't seen it up close before, and she pressed her nose to the glass along with Erin and Nora.

"Queen Victoria really wears this?" Lizzie asked. It was beautiful, dark but glossy, and fashioned into beads both smooth and faceted, oval brooches, teardrops, and even delicately carved cameos showing ladies' faces in profile. "It's like black amber."

Nora groaned theatrically. "I want it all. It's so beautiful. Dark and mysterious. I'd love to be dripping with jet."

"Hard to believe it was all just lying there buried in the ground." Hari seemed fascinated, to Lizzie's surprise. "Buried treasure."

"That necklace!" Nora jabbed her finger at a necklace like a waterfall of black droplets, draped over a velvet cloth.

Lizzie looked at her friend's pale skin and red hair. "You have just the right coloring for black jewelry," she said.

Hari nodded.

"Well, you do have a birthday coming up," Erin teased her sister. "We'll have to see what we can do. Wait, Lizzie, stop!"

The bell on the door rang loudly. The man behind the counter eyed Lizzie as she pushed her way in. "Anything I can help you with, love?"

Lizzie handed him a circus poster. "Stick that on your door?"

"Do I get free tickets if I do?"

"Don't need any. It's a free show." Lizzie hummed casually and strolled over to the window display. She tried to talk in a fancy voice. "I say, that's a handsome necklace there."

"You like it?" the shopkeeper asked her with a slight smile.

"Might I ask the price?"

He told her.

Spluttering, pale with shock, Lizzie pushed her way out of the shop without another word. "Don't ask," she gasped to her startled friends outside. "Just don't ask."

CHAPTER 5

The sun was lower in the sky by the time they finally reached the beach. There were still bathers all along its length; the women in one group, the men in another farther down. Lizzie stared at the strange wheeled huts that some of the bathers were using.

"They're bathing machines," Erin explained. "You can't have rich ladies getting changed and taking a dip in front of everyone, can you? Wouldn't be proper. So they hide inside those things."

"Are we going to get in trouble if we go in together?" Lizzie looked nervously at Hari, Malachy, and Dru. "Maybe the boys better go down to the other end."

Nora let out a *pfff* of scorn. "Leave all that foolishness to the grown-ups. Nobody's going to say anything to a bunch of kids."

"I hope not." Lizzie shuddered, glancing around in case a policeman or some other guardian of public morality was standing watch.

With nowhere else to change and no money for a bathing machine, the kids stood around in a circle facing outward and took turns putting their bathing suits on in the middle. Some of the wealthy ladies stared, but Nora and Erin just stared back until they lost their nerve.

I don't even have a bathing suit, Lizzie thought dismally. She'd just have to hitch up her skirts and paddle.

Finally, the Sullivan girls stood in all their glory, ready to go in. They wore long garments like striped sailor suits.

Nora hugged herself. "I look like a candy cane!" she moaned. "Let's just run into the sea before anyone sees us."

"Race you!" yelled Erin. She sprinted across the sand and went splashing into the water, shrieking at the cold. Nora followed, plowing through the surf and squealing as loudly as her sister.

Lizzie ran down to the edge of the whispering white surf, but stopped just before she reached it. Up ahead, the twins were throwing handfuls of water at one another and screaming. Lizzie dipped her toe in the sea and felt the delightful icy touch of the water splashing over her feet and washing up to her ankles. She wriggled her feet and felt her toes sinking in a little. What a peculiar, wonderful feeling. She stared, transfixed, at all the tiny bubbles in the seafoam.

Dru waded in, with Hari close behind, then Malachy, who left his crutch lying on the beach. "Just come in a little bit," Malachy suggested.

"In my clothes?"

"Why not?"

Lizzie sloshed her feet through the water and shook her head. "It's too cold."

"It's easier if you do it all at once," Mal told her. "You soon get used to it."

"I ain't ready yet!" Lizzie shouted, annoyed.

"Do I have to come and drag you in like an octopus?" Erin teased. "It's only the sea, you big baby. It won't bite you."

"Leave her alone," Malachy told her. "Let her do it in her own time."

Dru was already swimming back and forth along the shore, his long arms plunging under the waves with total confidence. Lizzie laughed at his huffing, puffing face every time it emerged from the water. He looked like a little mole.

Hari held out his hand, reminding Lizzie of the train and how scared she'd been of that. "We've come all this way to the sea, so come on in," he said. "It's nicer than you think."

"I don't know how to swim," Lizzie finally admitted, shamefaced. Standing there in her dress, with the waves up to her shins, she felt like a total fool. Everyone would laugh at her now, she knew it.

But Hari just smiled. "I see. Would you let me teach you, then?"

"Could . . . could you do that?"

"I can certainly try."

Hari led her into the deeper water, and Lizzie squealed as the cold bit into her legs and body. "It's freezing!"

Hari laughed in agreement. "I learned to swim in the Arabian Sea," he said. "It was a lot warmer than this."

While the others looked on and waved encouragingly, Hari patiently talked Lizzie through the basics. The cold water didn't seem so cold once she started moving around, kicking her legs and thrashing with her arms. Hari taught her to tread water first, and when she got the hang of that, she tried a dog paddle.

"Swim to me." Hari waded a little way farther out. "It's only a few feet. You can do this."

"Okay," Lizzie puffed. "Just watch me." Mustering all her willpower, she churned away at the water, kicking and scrabbling with her arms and — to her delight — realized she wasn't sinking. Lizzie swam with all her might and was so focused on Hari that she only saw the huge wave rearing up behind him after it was too late.

She shrieked as the wave deluged them both. Salty water filled her mouth and nose. Moments later, she stood, coughing and spitting, her hair hanging down all around her. There was something wet and slimy in her face, tangled through her hair.

She picked it out. It was seaweed. Dru was watching her and, expecting him to laugh, she got ready to fling it at him in anger.

But he didn't laugh. "You look like a mermaid, Lizzie," he said gallantly.

She turned away. "Ugh. I'm covered in goose bumps. I'm ready to dry off."

* * *

Nobody had any towels, so after they climbed out of the water, everyone lay on the beach in the strong late summer sunshine, talking quietly and letting the sun dry them. Lizzie couldn't remember ever having felt more at peace. "I don't want to get up ever again," she sighed. "I'll lie here until I starve to death."

"No need to starve," Malachy said. "There's a girl who sells seafood not far from here."

Dru sat up. *"Perfect!* My treat."

Before Lizzie could stop him, Dru put his fingers in his mouth and blew a shrill whistle, which brought the girl running. She was Lizzie's age, with curly hair as black as Whitby jet. A tray hung around her neck from a leather strap. Her polite smile changed to a more honest grin when she drew close and saw them all together.

"You look like trouble," she joked. "You'd better have money. If you think I'm giving these away, you're wrong."

"Bien sûr!" Dru said, pretending to be offended.

At the sound of his accent, the girl turned a little pink and giggled. "Very well, *monsieur.* What'll it be?"

Dru bought some clams to share. He immediately dug into the pile on his plate. Lizzie stared at the strange slimy things, wondering if she could eat a food so odd-looking, but they turned out to be delicious, despite looking like something Akula might sneeze up.

The girl stayed to talk. Her name, they soon learned, was Elsie. When she asked innocently if they were servants for a rich family on vacation in Whitby, the Penny Gaff Gang grinned at one another, wondering who should be the one to explain.

"We're with the circus," Lizzie eventually said.

"Get out!"

To prove it, they showed her the posters Fitzy had given them to hang and pointed out first Dru, then the twins. Elsie seemed star-struck after that, mumbling shyly, especially at Dru.

Lizzie tried to draw her out again. "It's lovely here," she said. "Beautiful and peaceful. Not like smelly old London. You're so lucky to live here by the sea."

"You reckon?" Elsie said, giving her an odd look. "Don't let the sunshine and seaside tomfoolery trick you. It's a different story after dark."

Lizzie felt the hairs on her scalp prickle. Maybe now she'd learn why she'd had a vision foretelling her arrival. "How d'you mean?"

"Whitby's haunted," Elsie said in a voice barely above a whisper.

"By who?"

"The ghosts of drowned sailors. Those who've died at sea. The fog comes rolling in, and they drift with it, up the beach and into the wet streets. If you're very quiet, you can hear them tap-tap-tappin' on the windows. They want their loved ones to come down and let them in. But you must never do that, or you'll be a cold corpse yourself come the morning."

Lizzie had fresh goosebumps on her arms when Elsie finished speaking. She knew ghosts were real. She'd seen them and spoken to them. Even though the story Elsie was spinning sounded like a fireside tale — the sort of thing children tried to spook one another with — it still reminded her of her vision.

"The sailors come on a ghost ship," Elsie went on. "It sails in on a cloud of mist, and from time to time, it takes living souls away, never to be seen again. Some say the captain is the devil himself."

Now Lizzie's spine was crawling. *A ghost ship? That's what I saw!*

"That's one of your local legends, is it?" Malachy asked.

"It's the gospel truth," Elsie insisted. "I've seen the ghost ship out at sea with my very own eyes."

Lizzie wanted to tell her to stop joking, but the fear in the girl's eyes was real. She believed what she was saying.

"Where from?" Malachy said, curious now.

"Our cottage up by the harbor," Elsie told him. "I saw it through my window, shrouded in mist, flickering with a strange light. I couldn't sleep because I kept thinking of it!" She stood up suddenly and brushed the sand off her dress. "Nice talking to you all, but I'll take my leave of you now, if you don't mind. I have work to do. Good day."

After eating their clams, the children strolled along the harbor. Dru darted off without warning, then came running up to Lizzie five minutes later. "I bought you a present," he gasped. "Some rock."

Lizzie laughed. "There's rock all over the place. On the beach, on the cliffs . . . you didn't need to pay for it."

"Not *this* sort of rock, *ma belle.*" Dru passed her a stick of something wrapped in paper. "This, you eat."

Lizzie unwrapped it, giving Dru suspicious glances, and took a test bite. An explosion of minty sweetness went off in her mouth. She rewarded him with a smile of pure delight.

Nora and Erin, meanwhile, were chatting with a man in a straw hat and striped jacket. He was tanned and handsome, and Lizzie thought that he looked Italian or even Greek. He stood behind a table draped with a blue cloth. Three shells had been set out on it.

"Oh, I know this trick," Lizzie told Dru. "One of Pa's friends used to do it. We need to warn 'em. He tricks you into thinking you know which shell the pea is under."

"I think Erin knows exactly what she's doing," Dru said.

"Now, my name's Billy," the man said. "What might your name be, sweetheart?"

"It might be Queen Titania," said Erin, hands on hips. "But it's not."

"Now you've clearly got the gift of the gab, my sweet girl, but do you have the luck of the Irish along with it?" Billy said. "I've got a shiny shilling here for you if you do. What's the catch, you ask? It's a penny in. That's all. Who wouldn't risk a penny to win a shilling, eh?"

"Listen to him talk!" Lizzie whispered.

Erin slapped a penny down on the table, and Billy started back with mock surprise. "Steady on, my duck, no need to start wrecking the place! Now, this is a game we call Find the Lady." He held up a dried pea, then put it down and clapped a shell over it, quickly nudging the other shells alongside it. "First time, this one's just for fun, not playing for money yet, keep your eyes on the prize . . ." His hands moved in a blur, swiveling the shells around one another in figure-eights and quick swaps. "Which one's it under?"

"That one!" Erin tapped the middle shell.

Billy lifted it, revealing the pea. "Oh, dear," he said. "Oh, Mother, I feel faint. I'm done for. She'll make a beggar of me. Ma always said the pretty girls would be my ruin. Another try? For the money this time?"

Erin laughed. "Why not."

But this time, to nobody's surprise, the pea wasn't where she'd thought it was. Erin stared in disbelief as Billy unveiled it, winked, and tucked her penny into his pocket. "Any time you want another go-round, my darling, just you come and find me."

"Where can I find you, then?" Erin said, cocking her head. Lizzie was startled to see her acting so bold and grown up all of a sudden.

"Walking back and forth upon the earth, and walking up and down on it." Billy tipped his hat.

Erin strolled back to join them, smiling and shaking her head.

"You're in a good mood for someone who's just lost money," Malachy challenged her.

"Ah, it was money well spent," said Erin. "He's an entertainer, just like us. Did you hear that patter of his? He's a master at it."

"Good hands, too," agreed Nora. "Fast."

"We should talk to Fitzy. Maybe he'd take Billy on," Erin suggested. "We could use a showman like him."

"Not a chance," Malachy said. He sounded angry. "My dad doesn't hire shysters and con men. Billy can stay down here where he belongs."

"Come on, Nora," Erin said. "Let's walk a bit more."

As they strolled off, chatting casually and giggling, Malachy glared after them.

Lizzie nudged Dru. "She was flirtin' with him, wasn't she?" she whispered. "If her ma knew, she'd skin her alive!"

Dru laughed softly. "So don't tell her."

CHAPTER 6

The next day, a small crowd was gathered in the huge castle kitchens, including Johnson, the groundskeeper.

"Mrs. Cobbett isn't going to like it, sir," Johnson told the Maharaja.

"My dear man, Mrs. Cobbett is being given the whole afternoon and evening off, as are the rest of the kitchen staff," the Maharaja said. "She has nothing to complain about."

"But that's her kitchen," Johnson insisted. "She won't want strangers in it."

"I can hardly ask Mrs. Sullivan to cater a picnic dinner for the whole of her circus cast and crew in her little tent, now can I?" the Maharaja said. He ushered Johnson out of the castle kitchens, past where Lizzie and the Sullivans stood waiting in the hallway. Johnson glowered at them as he passed.

Ma Sullivan took a deep breath. "Okay, girls! Let's get to work." She strode into the kitchens and looked around approvingly at the hanging pots and pans, the slate work surfaces, the colossal table, and the stove. All the walls were covered in cream-colored tiles with embossed patterns. "Would you look at the size of this place! I could feed five thousand with a kitchen like this."

"Why does the Maharaja think you couldn't cope in your tea tent?" Erin asked, casting a wary eye over the dangling ladles and knives. "You feed us all every day with your little stove."

"Ah, but not all at once, my love, and that's the point." Ma Sullivan rolled up her sleeves. "The Maharaja wants a grand feast, and a grand feast he shall have."

Just then, Flora, the circus's Fat Lady, and the tall woman known as the Amazon Queen let themselves into the kitchen.

"Heard it was all hands to the pump," Flora said. "What can we do to 'elp?"

"You heard right," Ma Sullivan said. "I'll need spuds peeled, chickens plucked, and apples cored. Anything these folks don't have in their supplies we'll have to send to town for."

That afternoon, it was Ma Sullivan who was the ringmaster, taking over the castle kitchens and ransacking the stores, while Nora, Erin, and Lizzie scurried around doing whatever they were told and trying not to get under anybody's feet. Lizzie did her best, but she wasn't used to cooking, and when she tried to chop an onion, it shot across the room like a cannonball. Taking the knife from her, Ma Sullivan sent Lizzie off on an errand instead.

"We'll need ice for the ice cream. You know where it's kept?"

"The ice house?" Lizzie guessed.

Ma Sullivan winked. "Smart girl."

Lizzie had seen the ice house earlier, a gloomy stone building like a tiny tomb, cold enough to store ice in the summer. As she crossed the lawn, she saw the castle staff setting up tables and chairs and laying delicate white cloths out.

It's going to be a fancy dinner party, Lizzie thought, feeling a surge of excitement. Tonight she'd dine with royalty. It was a long way from the squalor and hunger of Rat's Castle, where she'd first started out.

Johnson was ordering the rest of the staff around, grumpily instructing them to set a table down here or a chair there, and to watch out for the flowerbeds while they did it. As Lizzie watched, the Maharaja came strolling over in his hunting coat, smoking a fat cigar and nodding in approval.

"Good work, Johnson," he said.

"With respect, sir, you oughtn't to be hosting this party at all."

"Why on earth not?" the Maharaja asked.

"I'd be wary of showing off your wealth in front of all these strangers. I wouldn't let them into my home, neither. They don't have much, by the look of them, and envy can give people sticky fingers."

The Maharaja waved away the comment. "They are my guests. Now, you have your instructions, Mr. Johnson. I expect you to carry them out. Good man." He walked away, whistling to himself.

Johnson stared after him. He was turning beet red with anger again. "Marching around like he owns the bloomin' place, when he's only the tenant," he muttered. "He'll learn. Oh, he'll learn. 'From him who hath much, much shall be taken away.'"

Lizzie found Hari down by the ice house. Her friend was poking around in the gravel and jumped when he saw Lizzie.

"What are you up to?" she asked him.

"Just examining the local rocks," Hari said casually. "You can find lots of interesting fossils out here on the coast."

"Right," Lizzie said, eyeing him curiously. "What's so interesting about them?"

"They're the remains of ancient animals," Hari explained.

"Well, sorry to drag you away from your old animal rocks, but can you help me carry some ice to the kitchen?" Lizzie asked.

They each gathered up a block of ice from the dark, straw-packed cavity inside the building. "We should drop some of this down old Johnson's back," Lizzie said with a giggle. "Help him cool off."

"Is he shouting about his lawns again?" Hari asked.

"He's angry at the Maharaja for telling him what to do. I dunno why. He's a servant, ain't he? He gets paid to do what he's told."

"Some white people think brown people are meant to take orders, not give them," Hari said. "If someone with dark skin tells them what to do, it turns their whole world upside down."

Lizzie frowned. "I never even thought of that."

Hari shrugged. "Why would you? You're white."

"It must be hard for you and your uncle, looking different."

"Different," Hari said thoughtfully. "Do you know what they call brown-skinned people in India?"

"No, what?" Lizzie asked.

"People."

* * *

Later that afternoon, Ma Sullivan was in despair. "Lizzie, Lord love you, do you even know one end of a knife from another? I asked you to top and tail those green beans, and you've murdered them in cold blood!"

Lizzie, who'd held the kitchen knife with both hands and hacked at the beans like a maniac, was not discouraged. "I can still help. Just give me something else to do."

"Can you beat an egg white until it's stiff?" Ma Sullivan asked.

"Dunno," Lizzie said brightly. "Never tried."

Ma Sullivan heaved a sigh that seemed to come from the pit of her stomach. "Better not, then. I'm scared to think what might come of it. Tell you what, let's set you to buttering the bread. Lord help us if you can't manage that."

"'Course I can butter a slice of bread!" Lizzie scoffed.

Ma Sullivan set her to work and asked in a softer voice, "Did you never help with the cooking at home, love?"

Lizzie shrugged. "There wasn't ever much to cook, even when my ma was alive. Pa took all the money and spent it on drink."

"Mother of mercy," Ma Sullivan said, shaking her head. "No wonder you were all skin and bones when you joined up with Fitzy's." She whipped up egg whites and sugar into a foamy froth, then poured blobs of it out on a baking sheet.

Nora and Erin looked on excitedly. "Are you making meringues, Ma?"

"I am. We'll have whipped cream and cherries, and we can use some ice to make a blackberry sorbet."

Lizzie's mouth watered at the thought of a table laden with desserts. "How'd you know how to make all this fancy food?" she asked. "Cakes is one thing, but this is a bit classy, isn't it?"

"I used to be in service!" Ma Sullivan said proudly. Her kindly eyes crinkled with amusement. "Picture me in a fancy apron, if you will."

"Our ma worked in a big house like this one," Erin butted in. "The lord of the manor took a fancy to her when she was only eighteen, and it was ever so scandalous."

"That he did, and that it was, and I was having none of it, so I ran away," Ma Sullivan said. "Nora, would you check the red cabbage, it's boiling dry for heaven's sake. I met my dear Mr. Sullivan in a ballroom in Galway, back in Ireland. Before you could whistle, I'd run off to join the circus!" She laughed loudly over the sound of bubbling pots and rattling lids.

Lizzie loved hearing Ma Sullivan's stories — when the twins would let her finish them, that was. "Fitzy must have been a young man then."

Ma Sullivan shook her head. "No, this wasn't Fitzy's. We joined up with a fella name of Lovett — American, he was. Used to tour with a Wild West show, like Sean and the boys do now. We traveled with him for a while — Flora, see if the pantry's got a spare bottle of sherry for the trifle, and I'll have one myself while you're at it! — and then with a lot of other circuses until we joined Fitzy a few years ago."

"Do you ever miss it?" Lizzie asked. "Working in a big house?"

"Miss it? *Miss it?*" Ma Sullivan laughed until Lizzie worried she might hurt herself. "Oh, Lizzie, you do say the silliest things. Miss being bossed around by a bunch of snobs who look down on you all the time? Who could miss that?" She paused and looked around. "Ah, but a grand kitchen like this, it's wasted on the likes of Mrs. Cobbett. I could work wonders in this place."

CHAPTER 7

Months ago, when Dru had been arrested by the London police under the belief he was the mysterious Phantom burglar, Lizzie had brought the real villain to light and saved Dru's life. His sister, Collette, who had been icy and harsh with Lizzie before, changed her attitude overnight.

Her gratitude and affection had been a bit embarrassing at first, but still, Collette did know fashion. In thanks, she had given Lizzie a stunning dress she'd outgrown. It was meant to be for special occasions, but the garment was so beautiful that Lizzie had never worn it. She sometimes unfolded it, just to look at it, and then put it away again. She felt silly holding on to it.

When will I ever get a chance to dress up in fancy clothes living this circus life, constantly on the road? Lizzie had wondered on more than one occasion.

But tonight, she had finally found an occasion.

"It's time," Lizzie whispered, unfolding the package of brown paper. A waft of lavender went up; Collette had left some in the dress's folds to protect against moths.

The dress was blue silk, with a black lace overlay and beaded buttons. Lizzie changed into it, looked at herself in the mirror, and made a little excited noise in her throat. She wasn't sure how she would be able to eat with these butterflies in her stomach.

On impulse, Lizzie snatched up her mother's tortoiseshell comb and arranged it in her brown hair, just so. Perfect. "Time to go," she told her reflection. "Wish you could be here, too, Ma."

The sun was setting behind the turrets of Dunsley Castle when Lizzie made her way outside. All the circus folk were gathered on the lawn, dressed in their finest clothes. Lizzie stared at the clowns, unrecognizable in evening dress. She could tell that some last-minute sewing jobs had been carried out, and some collars had been freshened up with chalk, but at least they had made the effort.

Lizzie joined up with the twins, and she, Nora, and Erin slowly walked over to where Dru, Hari, and Malachy were standing below a tree. Nora and Erin were in identical dresses of rust-colored silk, their hair patiently combed through and tied up in bows. The boys all looked like young men in their evening clothes. A strange silence fell as they looked one another up and down.

Malachy coughed. "Erin, you look, um . . ."

Erin cocked her head. "Cat got your tongue?" she joked.

"You're all so . . ." Hari couldn't get the words out.

Nora raised an eyebrow and smirked.

Dru came to their rescue. "Ladies, you are all exquisite. It would be our honor if you would accompany us to the table. Gentlemen, *allons-y*."

He offered Lizzie his arm and she took it, her heart thumping. She felt very grown-up all of a sudden, acting like this.

The Maharaja spread his hands in welcome. He wore his full ceremonial ensemble, from the turban festooned with pearls to the great lengths of rich crimson silk that draped his arms and waist. But it was the woman behind him who drew everyone's attention — it was the same blond woman he'd been sitting with at the Oxford performance. Now she was dressed in deep indigo and wore so much black jet jewelry that it put the window display at Delingpole's to shame.

"My friend, the Lady Susannah de Montefiore," the Maharaja said proudly.

Everybody stood in a line, ready to be introduced to the pair, and a hubbub of whispered conversation began.

"She's so beautiful," Lizzie murmured to the Sullivans.

Ma Sullivan sucked at her cheeks. "Yes, she's a looker, and don't she know it?"

"Ma!" said Nora through clenched teeth.

"I speak as I find," Ma Sullivan said firmly. "She's a little too full of herself for my liking." She narrowed her eyes. "She reminds me of someone, too. Was it . . . no, can't place her. Probably one of the fancy people I used to work for. Lord knows there were enough of those."

Fitzy worked his way down the line, introducing the Maharaja to each member of the circus. The Maharaja shook their hands enthusiastically and seemed every bit as excited as he had been in the show tent. He was full of questions: *Did Mario the Mighty have a special diet? Was every clown's makeup truly unique? How old was Leo the lion?*

He was especially excited to meet Lizzie. "The famous fortune-teller! I tried palm reading myself, you know, but I never had the knack for it. Do you do séances? I've been to a few in London where a psychic communicated with spirits."

Lady Susannah, who had been quiet until now, spoke up before Lizzie could answer. "You're a clairvoyant?"

"Yes, ma'am," Lizzie said, giving a little curtsey. Was that the right thing to do? She had absolutely no idea.

"I'm sure you're very convincing," the lady said with a gracious smile. She turned to the Maharaja. "It's all an act, my love. They work it all out with special signals and so forth. She doesn't really have mysterious powers."

"She does," Hari insisted. "You should let her do a reading for you. You won't doubt her after that, I promise you."

"Well," Lady Susannah said with a light laugh, "perhaps that can be arranged."

"I love your jewelry!" Nora burst out, unable to contain herself. "It's just beautiful."

Erin glared at her sister, but Lady Susannah didn't seem to mind. "Jet is popular in London, too," she smiled. "For the same reason as séances are, I am sorry to say. Grief for the dead. Our beloved Queen Victoria is wearing it in mourning."

The Maharaja sighed. "Indeed. Poor, dear Victoria. Since her husband, Albert, passed away, she is quite inconsolable. I fear she will waste away altogether from sheer grief."

It gave Lizzie a giddy feeling to think that the man in front of her was a close friend of the Queen of England. "Poor thing," she said, not knowing what else to say.

"Don't tell the Queen," said the Maharaja with a wink, "but I have a gift I think will bring fire back into her heart again. Mum's the word, okay?"

Lizzie suddenly had a hunch. The word *sparkling* had popped into her mind. "Is it jet jewelry?" she guessed.

"Oh, no!" The Maharaja laughed, lifting a chubby finger. "My present is far more valuable than jet."

Lizzie noticed Lady Susannah giving him a somewhat frosty look, but said nothing. *Is the lady jealous of Queen Victoria?* she wondered. It must be a truly amazing present if that was the case . . .

The Maharaja moved on down the line, and Lady Susannah followed after him.

As the pair moved away, Nora sighed and muttered, "Look at all that jet. It's lying on her in piles! Oh, I'd do anything for some of my own!"

"You don't need jewelry," Hari said in a shy voice. "You're pretty enough as you are."

"I thought you only liked fossils?" Lizzie teased.

Nora hadn't heard properly and spun around indignantly. "Did you just call me a *fossil*, Hari?"

* * *

Later on, as they were about to sit down to dinner, Lizzie glanced out over the castle grounds. Dusk was setting in, but the sea was still dimly visible in the far distance. Just as she was fondly remembering how it felt to swim there, a strange greenish light appeared, flickering across the waves. It was only there for a second, and then it was gone.

Lizzie rubbed her eyes and looked again. *Probably just my imagination*, she thought. It had been a long, busy day after all.

But just then, the light flickered again. Was she seeing things, or was it really there, coming from a misty cloud on the sea?

A chill ran through Lizzie's body. She'd seen that sight in her vision, and now she was seeing it in real life. She remembered what Elsie had said about the ghosts of drowned sailors returning to the town after dark. The light she was seeing now must be the same light Elsie had spoken fearfully about — the light of the ghost ship.

CHAPTER 8

The next morning, Lizzie woke up in her wagon still feeling full. So it hadn't been a dream — she really had gorged herself on roast chicken, mashed potatoes, gravy, and tiny sweet peas, and then plate after plate of meringues drowning in thick cream and cherries as red as the Maharaja's ruby rings.

She sat up, noticing that her limbs still ached a little. Ah, yes. The dancing. The Maharaja had clapped his hands, the band had begun to play, and everyone had begun to dance in couples and singles across the lawns, around the tents, and in and out of the bushes, laughing as they went. Lizzie had joined in, along with Erin and Malachy, Hari and Nora, and Dru.

"Phew," Lizzie said, collapsing back against her mound of pillows. "It's good I ain't a princess. I don't reckon I've got the energy for it."

Her memories of the night before were a bit hazy, but she remembered still being up past one in the morning. No wonder she felt exhausted. *Tea*, she thought. *What I need is a nice, hot cup of tea.*

Lizzie quickly dressed and headed over to Ma Sullivan's catering tent. To her surprise, it was empty, with only Ma Sullivan herself waiting behind the counter.

"She's alive!" Ma Sullivan exclaimed with a laugh. "It's a miracle."

"Where is everybody? What time is it?" Lizzie asked.

"It'll be about eight o'clock, my dear. Everybody's already up and rehearsing. Tea and toast?"

"Just tea, thanks. I don't think I'll need to eat again for about a week."

Lizzie took a seat, and soon Ma Sullivan brought tea over for them both. "I'm not in trouble, am I?" Lizzie asked. "For sleeping in?"

"Oh, bless you, no," Ma Sullivan reassured her. "You're not in the show. It's only the performers who are at work already. They want to make this show really special for the Maharaja, you see. He's already seen the regular routine back in Oxford, so they're trying to work out some new stunts."

"Oh. I don't have much to do today, then," Lizzie said. She thought for a moment. "I know! I could help you make a birthday cake for Erin and Nora!"

"That's sweet of you, dear, but it's all under control. I wouldn't want to put you to the trouble." Ma smiled in a sly way. "Now if I was in your shoes, I'd be finishing what I started last night."

Lizzie gulped. "Finishing what?"

72

"Oh, don't make out like you don't know what I'm talking about. I saw you and Dru dancing the night away, out under the stars."

"So? All we did was have a dance!" Lizzie exclaimed. "Shame on you for teasing me!"

"You think I don't remember what it's like to be young?" Ma Sullivan winked.

"We're just friends," Lizzie insisted. "Can't friends have a dance together?"

Ma Sullivan laughed like a horse. "There's none so blind as those that will not see! Go on, be off with you. Go make yourself useful in the show tent."

Lizzie finished her tea before she left. It gave her a warm feeling inside, just like Ma Sullivan's laughter did.

When she slipped, unseen, into the show tent a few moments later, rehearsals were underway, each group in its own area. The clowns had one corner, the acrobats another, and up above on the high wire, Dru and Collette were polishing their routine.

Lizzie quietly took a seat at the back. Dru went promenading up and down the tightrope in a bathing suit, carrying his sister on his shoulders. Collette carried a parasol, which she twirled like a giant wheel, catching the light. By the look of it, they had revamped their act to give it a seaside theme.

That should give the locals a smile, Lizzie thought to herself.

Dru paused in the middle of the tightrope. His father, Pierre, sporting a fine black moustache curled up at the ends, threw him a stick of rock, followed rapidly by two more. Dru juggled the rock sticks, wobbling back and forth, while Collette snatched at them, never quite managing to get one.

I know what gave you that idea, Lizzie thought happily.

"Excuse me? Everyone? May I please have your attention?" It was the Maharaja, wringing his hands and standing in the entrance to the tent. "Something terrible has happened."

As soon as the circus folk saw the distraught look on his face, they stopped what they were doing and turned to listen. Dru deftly caught all three rock sticks in the same hand and hurried to the end of the wire, where he set Collette down with infinite care.

Lizzie could feel a hard lump of fear growing in her throat. The Maharaja looked dark-eyed and sick. His shirt was hanging out.

Someone's been murdered, Lizzie thought. *Or found dead in their bed, a cold corpse in the morning. That light I saw last night . . . Elsie tried to warn us about ghosts coming up from the harbor.* She told herself not to get carried away. Whatever might be going on, she should listen and help. That was what her powers were for, wasn't it?

"There's been a b-b-burglary," the Maharaja stammered. "L-l-last night, while Lady Susannah was sound asleep in her bedchamber, her jet jewelry was stolen."

Everyone looked at each other uneasily. There were a few murmurs and gasps; some of the circus people looked weary and miserable, as if they'd known this was all too good to last.

Lizzie felt that way, too. It had all been going too well. Even though Johnson was wary of them, they'd been made welcome here. And now this . . .

"I have to ask," the Maharaja went on, "if anyone here saw anything suspicious after the dinner party. Anything at all."

Here we go again, Lizzie thought with a heavy heart. Even though she'd only been in the circus a short while, she had quickly learned that many people had a low opinion of circus folk. Most assumed they were all criminals. She'd never forget the London policemen who had treated her like a thief on sight.

One of the clowns, Didi, spoke with a voice shaking with anger. "If we'd seen anything suspicious, sir, I expect we'd have said so at the time." He looked around. "I think I speak for all of us."

The Maharaja realized what Didi was upset about and quickly reassured him. "My dear man, I don't mean any offense. I am quite sure nobody here is involved in this dreadful deed. I am simply asking for your help in catching the culprit."

That took the wind out of Didi's sails. "Ah. Well, I do beg your pardon. We'll all keep our eyes open, won't we, fellas?"

A chorus of "yes!" and "of course!" was his answer.

"I am in your debt, my friends," the Maharaja said. "Any detail you might recall, however insignificant it might seem, could be of help. Everyone told me Whitby was cursed, but I laughed in their faces. How I wish I had not. My poor Lady Susannah is quite beside herself with grief."

I bet she is, Lizzie thought. The lady had been so proud of her jewels. Maybe whoever had taken them had been jealous of her wealth or wanted to humble her. Someone from her past, perhaps?

As the Maharaja turned to leave, Lizzie stood up and called "Wait!" at the top of her voice. She ran down to the startled man.

"Yes? You saw something, my dear?"

"No," Lizzie gasped, "but I might."

The Maharaja looked blank.

"I could read her palm," Lizzie explained. "I see things. I might have a vision of what really happened. Who it was that did it."

The Maharaja didn't seem to know what to say to that. "Thank you," he eventually said, with great respect. "I will pass on your kind offer to Lady Susannah. She is far too upset right now, but when she calms down, perhaps you could offer to do . . . whatever it is you do."

Once the Maharaja had gone, Hari went and sat next to Lizzie. "You're really going to help him?"

"Of course," Lizzie said. "Why wouldn't I?"

"I always thought your powers were meant to be used for good," Hari said. There was a coldness in his voice that Lizzie didn't like.

"I feel sorry for him and for Lady Susannah. It ain't nice to have your stuff stolen, is it?"

Hari laughed bitterly. "Have you ever heard of *karma*, Lizzie?"

"Can't say I have."

"There's a saying you English have that sums it up pretty well: 'What goes around, comes around.' I'm not going to be crying any tears for the Maharaja having his jewels stolen," Hari said. "Not when he's stolen jewels from his people in India!"

"'Scuse me," Lizzie said, confused at his attitude. "I'm . . . I'm going for a walk." She strode off, feeling like everything was turning sour all of a sudden. Maybe the circus would have been better off setting up in Reading after all.

Out on the lawn, the tables and chairs were still set out from the previous night's party, though they were bare now. Nora was sitting there alone, her arms flat on the tabletop, her head resting on the backs of her hands. Lizzie thought she was asleep until she saw her friend's eyes were open. She was gazing up at the castle.

"What are you up to?" Lizzie asked, sitting down next to her friend.

"Wondering which one is her window," Nora said with a sigh.

"I hate this," Lizzie said. "It was supposed to be so much fun. The Maharaja's just tryin' to cheer everyone up, and now this happens!"

"Poor Lady Susannah," said Nora. "That jewelry was so gorgeous."

"Jet costs a ton," Lizzie agreed, remembering Delingpole's.

"I know." Nora sighed again. "But it's not just that, is it? It was a gift from him. From her handsome prince."

"I didn't even think of that." *Nora is surprisingly romantic sometimes*, Lizzie thought. Her friend dreamed of castles and fairy-tale weddings. She was so different from Erin, who made rude jokes and flirted with con men on the sea front. Although the twins looked identical, their personalities were complete opposites.

"So, who do you think did it?" Nora asked. "You must have had a vision or something. You're always getting them over stuff like this."

"I haven't a clue!" Lizzie said, shaking her head. "No visions, no dreams, nothing."

Nora frowned in thought. "It must have been someone who could have gotten inside the castle," she announced, sounding like a detective making a clever deduction.

"Well, that could have been anyone!" Lizzie scoffed. "There's no security here to speak of, is there?"

"Suppose not."

"The Maharaja is like a great big, cuddly sheepdog. He thinks everyone's his friend. He's just too trusting."

Nora's lip trembled. "Why did this have to happen, Lizzie? Why can't things just be . . . just be *nice?*"

Lizzie put a comforting arm around her friend's shoulder. But the second her body touched Nora's, a vision exploded into her mind, as sudden and forceful as a blow to the face. She whimpered and clutched her forehead, her fingers jerking as if trying to rip the unwanted vision out of her mind and fling it away.

"Lizzie?" Nora gasped. She pulled away. "What can you see?"

"I . . ." She stopped. She couldn't tell her. The vision was still there, fixed in her mind like a nightmare that wouldn't fade even after waking.

In her mind's eye, she saw Nora. She was holding her long hair out of the way and fastening a stunning necklace around her neck — a necklace made of rich, black jet.

"Are you all right?" Nora asked, looking concerned. "Do you want a drink of water?"

"Would you mind?" Lizzie croaked. "I'll wait here. Thanks."

As Nora ran off, Lizzie sat feeling sick to her stomach. She didn't really want a drink — she'd just needed to make

Nora go away, at least until that horrible vision was out of her head.

You know what it means, a nasty voice whispered at the back of her mind.

"I don't believe it," Lizzie muttered to herself. But an idea was taking shape in her imagination, even though she hated it. Nora had pined after that jet necklace like a lovesick schoolgirl. She'd gazed into the window at Delingpole's, talking about how much she wanted jet jewelry of her own.

Could she have stolen it? Lizzie wondered.

She thought back to how Nora had been only minutes before. Had she been staring at the window out of guilt? When she asked Lizzie if she'd had a vision, had there been a touch of panic in her voice — as if she feared she'd be found out?

"Stop it!" Lizzie scolded aloud. She smacked herself on the side of the head, hard enough to hurt. That brought her to her senses.

Mercifully, the vision began to fade and Lizzie felt dreadful now. Nora had become like a sister to her. She'd never had a best friend before. Nora was utterly loyal, kindhearted, and trusting. She'd *never* steal, no matter how much she coveted something that belonged to someone else.

"Feeling any better?" Nora asked when she returned. She passed Lizzie her glass of water.

"Much," said Lizzie, forcing a smile.

But a cold sense of worry was still looping deep down in her stomach. No matter how much she might trust Nora, Lizzie knew her visions had never been wrong before. Even Malachy had admitted it. She looked up into her friend's troubled, concerned face and wished she could say what was in her heart.

CHAPTER 9

Later that day, when the Penny Gaff Gang gathered in the gardens before their second trip into Whitby, Hari was reluctant to go.

"Come on, Hari, stretch your legs! It'll be fun!" Erin pleaded, tugging at Hari's arm. Lizzie wondered if she meant to drag him all the way to Whitby.

"I can't," Hari insisted. "I told you, I have chores to do."

"But we're at the seaside!"

"You could always help me clean out the lion cage if you want." Hari said. "My uncle will gladly give you a shovel."

Erin sighed and let go of his arm. "I don't know what's gotten into you lot. Yesterday you couldn't wait to get down to Whitby. Today you're in a foul mood."

"Everyone's just worn out after rehearsal and last night, probably," Lizzie said. "The sea air'll soon freshen us all up."

"It's not the sea air that Erin's looking forward to," Nora said, grinning and giving Lizzie a nudge. Lizzie smiled back, sharing the joke, but still felt awkward around Nora, which in turn made her feel horrible for feeling awkward.

As the rest of the Penny Gaff Gang headed toward the coast road and Whitby, Lizzie looked out toward the sea and wondered what secrets were hiding out there. How could such a bright, sunlit place be so creepy and mysterious after dark? Looking at the sea now, legends of ghost ships and supernatural mists seemed crazy.

But she hadn't imagined seeing that green light last night, nor the fog bank. Whether they were the work of ghosts or not, they were real.

Lizzie struggled to think of another explanation. An ordinary ship might shine a light, but a *green* one? Maybe she should ask the Maharaja if she could watch from one of the castle's towers and get a better view. She looked over her shoulder back toward Dunsley Castle, and to her surprise saw a dark-skinned figure hurrying away from the grounds.

Whoever it was seemed to be heading straight for the moors.

Lizzie squinted. Was that Hari? Why would he lie about needing to stay behind at the circus? Lizzie puzzled over that for a while. Perhaps he just needed to spend some time alone. After all, there wasn't much privacy to be had when you were part of a circus. Hari didn't even have his own wagon.

Besides, Lizzie thought as she saw Johnson the gardener digging in his flowerbeds, *there are plenty of people here that Hari probably wants to stay away from.*

Johnson raised his head as they approached. "Make sure you stay away from these rosebeds!" he shouted. "Prize-winners, they are. Not that the likes of you would care."

"We're not going anywhere near your flowers!" Lizzie shouted back angrily. It was true, obviously so. They weren't even heading in that direction.

Erin stuck out her jaw and gave Johnson a poisonous glare. Lizzie thought she might go and jump right in the middle of the flowerbeds, just to give old Johnson a heart attack. But Erin respected Fitzy, and Fitzy had promised they'd respect the gardens.

"We're going to the harbor," Erin said, turning her back on him.

"Is that so?" Johnson snarled. "You'd best be back before dark. Else you might be spirited away like the others before you."

Lizzie turned to say something ugly in reply but felt Malachy's arm leading her off. "Just walk away," he said quietly. "It's the best thing to do, always."

Lizzie went with him. "Sorry, Mal. These threats . . . it just makes me so angry."

Everywhere the circus went, they met distrust and suspicion. Lizzie hated it. Nobody in her life had been kinder to her than the people of Fitzy's Circus. Nobody deserved this treatment less than they did.

* * *

Lizzie stayed in a black mood for the rest of the walk to Whitby. The noonday sun was fierce, and there were no clouds to give any relief. The road, which must have been muddy not long ago, was baked to a dusty crisp.

She lagged behind the others and kicked loose stones off into the shrubbery. If it hadn't been for the lure of the sea, she'd have turned around and gone back to tell Johnson exactly what she thought of him. But she did want to swim again, even if it meant wading in wearing her clothes like yesterday. She'd never need to be afraid of the water again if only she could learn how to swim.

The welcome sight of the sea shimmering in the distance blew Lizzie's bad mood away like so much smoke. She couldn't stay in a sulk with all that beautiful water out there. Already it seemed less threatening than it had the day before.

"Hari is not here," Dru said, noticing her smile. "Perhaps you will let me be your swimming teacher today?"

"I think I'll be fine on my own," Lizzie said, feeling awkward. After their dance on the lawn, a swimming lesson would just be too much. Besides, she didn't want him to help her. She'd show him what a fast learner she was on her own.

Soon everyone was hurrying down the zigzag steps and onto the beach. A great stripe of glistening sand lay before them, unspoiled by footprints. Gulls strutted back and forth on the cliff above, waiting for some dropped morsel.

Lizzie took her shoes and socks off, wishing again that she had a proper bathing suit to wear and wondering how much they cost. The sand squished beneath her feet delightfully. She was glad to see fewer people were here this time. They had this whole stretch of beach to themselves.

Well, almost. Someone was sitting on the wall built to stop waves, his arm around a young blond woman. Lizzie recognized his striped jacket at once. "Isn't that Billy?" she asked. "The guy who did the pea and shell game yesterday?"

"It is!" Malachy agreed with a mixed chuckle and snort.

"Doesn't look like him to me." Erin sniffed and turned her back on the couple. "Are we going swimming or aren't we?"

But Lizzie was still watching. Billy — it was definitely him — turned to give the blond woman a kiss. Lizzie gasped and ran to Erin's side. "He's got a girl. Billy's kissing someone! Here, Erin, your beau's been snapped up."

Erin shrugged, pretending not to care. "So? He was too old for me anyway."

"Of course he was," Malachy said, suddenly sounding more cheerful. "Good thing you didn't talk my dad into taking him on. Imagine if you had."

"You sure you're all right?" Nora asked her sister. She touched her arm, but Erin swatted it away.

"I said I was fine!" she said a little snappily.

"Never mind, Erin," Lizzie said. With a wicked grin, she bent over and scooped up a starfish that was lying in a rock pool at her feet and chucked it at Erin. "There's plenty more fish in the sea!"

Erin caught the starfish reflexively, not realizing what it was. As it wriggled in her hands, she let out a shriek and dropped it. "Oh, you little *devil!* I'll get you!"

"Got to catch me first!" Lizzie called, laughing. She raced into the sea, knowing full well that Erin wouldn't follow her until she'd changed into her bathing suit. Then she stood with the sea foaming around her shins, sticking her tongue out, while Erin fumed and flapped and finally started laughing, too.

By the time she looked back up the beach, Billy and his girl had quietly slipped away.

Good, Lizzie thought. *I don't care what Erin says. She doesn't need to see you two kissing in front of her.* She felt a little odd, though, standing in the sea all by herself, so she began to wander up the beach while Erin and Nora changed into their bathing suits. She'd only gone a few steps when a gleam caught her eye.

Lizzie bent down and saw it was half an oyster shell, rough on one side but pearly and smooth on the other. *It might not be jet*, she thought, *but it's pretty*. If she cut and shaped the pearly part, it could make a lovely bracelet — the sort of thing a mermaid might wear.

Encouraged, Lizzie hunted for more shells and found the beach was rich with them. Her pockets were soon bulging with shells, not just from oysters but from scallops and snails, too. There'd be enough to make matching bracelets for both Erin and Nora for their upcoming birthday.

"What are you up to?" Nora asked, suddenly appearing by Lizzie's side with the rest of the gang.

Lizzie stood up straight. "Just beachcombing," she said casually.

"Coming for a swim?" Nora asked. She dived, her feet kicking up water behind her, and swam under the surface. Lizzie watched her bob up again, further out to sea, gasping and triumphant. "It's nice once you're under!" she called.

"Okay, then," Lizzie muttered to herself. "I did it yesterday, I can do it today." She sloshed away from the shore, gradually submerging herself up to her shoulders. From the shore, Malachy and Dru waved and cheered, egging her on.

Lizzie was up to her neck now. She took a deep breath and ducked her whole head under the water, thinking, *If I do it on purpose, it won't be so bad.*

Everything sounded funny underwater. All she could hear were sloshes and gurgles. Quickly, before she panicked, Lizzie burst up to the surface again.

"You're getting the hang of this!" Malachy called, clearly impressed. "Wish Hari was here to see it."

Dru waded in and did a lazy backstroke for a few yards. "She was swimming yesterday!" he called. "Not just wading. Perhaps today, she does not feel up to it."

His teasing spurred Lizzie on. She lifted her feet from the seabed and dog-paddled for all she was worth, swimming past her group of friends and close to where Dru was splashing. She wondered if he was impressed, but she couldn't tell. All her effort went into propelling herself forward.

The water below her swirled and rushed past, pulling her further out to sea. *I can handle this*, Lizzie thought. *I'm really swimming. If only Hari could see me now!*

There were no other swimmers in sight now, and the only thing Lizzie could see out this far were boats. She decided it was time to stop. The undertow had pulled her out a lot farther than she'd meant to come.

She put her feet down, expecting to find the sandy seabed. Her feet went down . . . and down. As if she'd missed a step going downstairs, they plunged into nothing.

I've gone too far out, Lizzie thought in sudden terror. *The water's deep here.*

She floundered, gasping, only just managing to keep her head above water. *Remember what Hari showed you,* she thought. *Tread the water, circle your arms, try not to panic.*

But just then a bright crescent of pain split Lizzie's head in two as if an axe had struck her. Not a cramp but a vision, forcing itself behind her eyes at the worst possible time.

"No!" Lizzie gasped as she tried to shut it out. But there was no fighting the vision. It overwhelmed her, the image taking over like a scary illustration from a book of ghost stories.

In her mind she saw a ship of some kind, with a single mast, looming out of a thick, white mist. A sickly green light blazed from the prow, casting eerie shadows across the dark waves. Dimly visible through the mist was a figure — the pilot of this strange vessel.

Lizzie didn't want to look, but her mind's eye swept closer anyway. The figure was wearing a ragged robe, like a hooded specter from a stage play. It raised its arms, and from the depths of its black hood, Lizzie saw two gleaming lights like eyes staring back at her.

The stories were real — a ghost ship, captained by Death himself.

Lizzie opened her mouth to scream, and the ocean flooded in. Salt water choked her. Struggling, her strength fading with every second, she sank beneath the water's surface.

The shadow on the ghost ship, still visible in her mind, reached its tattered arms out to grasp her . . .

CHAPTER 10

Images flashed before Lizzie's eyes. *So*, she thought distantly, *it's true what they say about drowning. You really do see your whole life unfolding in front of you.*

She saw her brother sitting up in bed, coughing blood into a handkerchief. Other memories followed, blindingly fast: her mother hugging her from behind when she was only three; her father roaring drunk and smacking her hard in the face; the Penny Gaff Gang gathered for lunch in the tea tent and laughing together.

"Lizzie!"

The voice seemed to come from far away, a place of dancing light and blue skies. Lizzie thought it might be her mother, calling her to join her in heaven. Blurry white shapes soared past above her head, above the waves. Were they angels? The next moment, a shadow moved into view.

"Lizzie, come on!"

Sorry, Mum, Lizzie decided. *I'm not ready for heaven just yet.*

She kicked hard, remembering everything Hari had told her, and tore at the water with her arms. Her chest felt like it would explode, but she fought and fought, heaving herself up until with a spluttering gasp she broke the surface.

Only feet away from her, Elsie the fishergirl was holding out her hand. She was hanging over the edge of a small boat. That was what had made the shadow.

"Take my hand, Lizzie!" Elsie called. "I won't let go."

Lizzie clutched for Elsie's hand, held it tight, and let the girl haul her on board. Elsie had strong brown arms, more powerful than they looked. A lifetime of hauling up fishing nets must have given her those muscles.

Lizzie spat salt water over the side of the boat, coughed, and slumped in the seat. The wood below her was hot from the sun. "Thanks," she managed to gasp.

All around the boat, the rest of the Penny Gaff Gang gathered. They clung onto the side and looked at her. "Is she okay?" Dru demanded.

"I'm fine," Lizzie said weakly. *That'll teach me*, she thought. *Try to show off in front of a boy and see where it gets you.*

"Climb aboard, everyone," Elsie said. "Let's get her back to the shore."

"You're an angel," Lizzie groaned. "I had a vision . . ."

Elsie paused, her hands on the oars. "What's she saying?"

"Elsie, can you show us to a tea shop or something?" Malachy said, giving the others a *you-know-what-I-mean* look. "If Lizzie's had one of her funny turns, she needs to sit down and have a nice hot cup of tea, somewhere people can't listen in."

Elsie looked puzzled, but curious. "Let's go and fetch your clothes off the beach. Then I'll take you back to our cottage. I knew there was more to you all than meets the eye."

* * *

Not long after, they were all crowded around the table in a tiny kitchen cluttered with fishing nets and lobster pots. Elsie's cottage was right beside the harbor, so close that you could look out across the sea through the diamond-leaded windows. A cat lounged there, basking in the sun and looking so peaceful Lizzie wondered if it had been stuffed.

Lizzie held her mug of tea in both hands and breathed in the steam. She was still shaking and felt deep-down cold, despite the fire Elsie had built from what little coal she had.

"You swam out too far," Dru scolded her. "That is how people drown, *ma cherie*. One strong cramp and — *boum!* Under the waves they go."

"I told you, I didn't get no cramp. I had a vision!"

"I thought that's what you said!" Elsie burst out. "You see things, don't you? Yesterday, when I was telling you about how Whitby's haunted, I thought you was laughing

94

at me. But you're like my auntie, aren't you? She had the sight."

"That's about the gist of it," Lizzie said, grateful she wouldn't have to explain everything all over again. "I tell fortunes at the circus. Only they're real fortunes, not made-up ones."

"So what did you see?" Nora seemed eager and excited. "Was it about what happened at the castle?"

Oh, why did you have to say that? Lizzie thought. *I'm trying not to think of you as a suspect as it is!*

"It was a ship," she said. "With a green light coming off it, and all this fog rolling around it like a great cloud."

Next to her, Elsie sucked in a sharp breath, and Lizzie paused, wondering if she should go on. After all, she didn't want to scare the girl. But Elsie had a right to know what was going on in her town, so Lizzie continued. "There was a figure steering the boat. It was horrible — it had this long black robe, and a hood, and these two shining spots inside, like a cat's eyes."

A frightened silence settled on the group around the table. By the window, the cat stretched, yawned, got up, and trotted away. The sun had gone dim, and dark clouds were rolling in from the east.

"You saw the ghost ship!" Elsie said. "That's what I see, night after night. I never saw the *thing* at the helm, though."

"Lucky you."

"Do you think it was a ghost?" Elsie asked.

"I don't know what it was." Lizzie shuddered. She couldn't get the memory out of her head. The way that hooded form had turned to the left and right, as if it were searching the sea . . . maybe Elsie's legend was true, and it was hunting for a living soul to snatch away.

"Sounds like it was wearing a shroud," Erin said. "In County Mayo, where my grandma lives in Ireland, there was a man who lived by the churchyard. Every night a lady came to visit him in a long white gown. When he finally plucked up the courage to kiss her, he saw that her gown was really a shroud! She'd been dead for over a hundred years!"

"That's nothing," Malachy said. "A knife-thrower who used to be with Fitzy's circus was haunted by the ghost of a man missing both his hands. It made him so scared of making a mistake he quit the circus and became a butcher!"

Soon they were all trading ghost stories around the table. It was funny how frightening each other on purpose was better than being frightened by something from outside.

The minutes ticked by. Outside the window, the sky grew steadily darker. Something covered in fur pressed up against Lizzie's ankles, and she started. A mew came from beneath the table, and she realized it was only Elsie's cat.

"Sorry about this," Elsie said. "Horatio wants feeding."

"Horatio?" Lizzie laughed.

"Named him after Admiral Nelson, the great war hero. I usually give him a bit of mackerel around three."

"It's three o'clock already?" Erin sprang out of her seat. "We're going to be late for rehearsal!"

As they barged out of the little cottage and into the street, the first wet drops began to fall. The sky was completely clouded over now, and the people going by hurried their steps.

Elsie stared up. "Would you look at that sky! It's black as night."

"So much for our lovely day out at the beach,"said Erin.

"We're going to get soaked," Lizzie said miserably. "And I only just dried off, too."

Dru sighed. "Well, we can't get there any faster by crying about it. Perhaps we should send for a carriage?"

Elsie laughed sharply. "Are you made of money, Mister Frenchie?" Then, as if she regretted the jibe, she gave them a sly smile and ushered them back indoors. "There's a way you could stay mostly dry, and it's better than any old carriage. But you'd have to promise not to tell."

"I promise," Lizzie said right away.

Elsie smiled to see her solemn face. "It's not *that* grave a business. Not nowadays. But in my grandad's day, people around here would've cut your throat if you blabbed about the Rum Road."

Lizzie was completely confused. "What's a rum road?" she asked.

Nobody seemed to have any idea — except Malachy, who was suddenly grinning broadly. "If it's what I think it is," he whispered to Lizzie, "I've wanted to see one all my life."

Elsie fetched a candle and led them through the rainy streets to a nearby pub, the Whitby Oyster. But instead of going inside, she took them around the back to the yard. Malachy grinned with excitement while everyone else looked confused.

Lizzie glanced around. She couldn't see any roads leading out of here. There was just a little cobbled area with some stalls for horses and a shabby wooden outhouse set against the side of the hill. To her amazement, though, Elsie opened the outhouse door, sparked the candle alight, and beckoned them all to come and see.

Lizzie came closer, and her jaw fell open. Instead of a nasty-smelling space with a plank over a hole, she saw a rough tunnel leading all the way into the hillside. The candle cast its unsteady light over the crude timbers propping the roof up and the ragged spider webs in their corners. It didn't look safe at all. In fact, it looked like something desperate men had hacked out of the earth in a hurry.

"I knew it!" Malachy crowed. "It's a smugglers' tunnel, isn't it?"

Elsie held a finger to her lips and winked. "Hush. Many folk have gone missing, never to be seen again, just for blurting out our secrets."

"Sorry."

"Follow it all the way to the end," Elsie told them. "It comes out in a thicket not far from Dunsley Castle, within spitting distance of the road. That's where the wagons used to wait."

"It goes *that* far?" Malachy peered into the darkness. "That's over half a mile. Fantastic!"

Elsie passed Lizzie the candle. Lizzie cupped her hand around the fitful light, wishing they had a real lantern to keep it safe. "Thanks," she said. "You will come and see the circus, won't you?"

"'Course I will!" The local girl paused. "Did you really mean it about being a real fortune-teller?"

Lizzie nodded.

"There's something I need to know for sure," Elsie said. "I'll come and ask you. You all be careful in that tunnel."

"It does look a bit unsteady," Nora said. "Should have got some honest Irish workers on the job. It'd stand till Doomsday then."

Elsie shook her head. "I don't mean that. Whitby's a haunted place. You have to watch out if you're going into the dark. You never know what's waiting there." Then, just as suddenly as the first time they'd met, she bade them goodbye and was out of sight in a second. Lizzie had the strangest feeling that Elsie might be a ghost herself.

The Penny Gaff Gang moved into the tunnel, looking around at the crumbling, cobwebbed walls and the few signs of people who'd been there before them: broken bottles, a smashed wooden box, and a couple of old bones.

Dru poked at the bones with his foot. "These are chewed, see?"

"Smugglers probably had dogs," Malachy said. "To keep watch." He sniffed. "That's funny. I could swear I can smell gunpowder."

"Gunpowder?" Erin and Nora said, amazed.

"Remember that routine the clowns did last year, with the firecrackers? That's how they smelled. The smugglers must have kept a stash of powder here."

"Last one in close the door behind you," Lizzie murmured. She held the candle up and edged her way forward, the darkness opening up before her and returning silently in her wake. The rest of the gang followed, marveling at the spooky atmosphere.

"We must be right under the town!" Erin said. "Imagine if we were going under a graveyard right now. And a skeleton put its foot through the roof."

"Oh, hush up," Lizzie said. The air down here was musty and damp, and it was all too easy to imagine ghosts up ahead, rushing toward them out of the black, their bony arms clawing. She tried to think of the living people who had used this tunnel, not the ghosts who might be haunting it. "Why's it called a Rum Road?"

"Because this is how they brought the rum inland," Malachy explained. "Tobacco, too, and fancy lace. Stuff like that. But mostly rum."

"I still don't get it."

"Lizzie, if you bring rum into the country on a ship, you have to pay a special tax. It's called the excise. But they can't make you pay it unless they catch you with the goods. So they have special patrols looking out for anyone trying to smuggle it in."

Suddenly it made sense. "So this tunnel is for dodging the patrols!"

"Exactly." Malachy ducked under an enormous spider dangling from a glistening thread. "The smugglers could bring the rum ashore, right under the noses of the excise men."

"What do you think, Lizzie?" asked Dru. "Are the tunnels really haunted?"

Lizzie shrugged. "Elsie thinks so. I ain't about to argue with her."

"Whoooo!" Erin hooted, wiggling her fingers in the candlelight to make long, spooky shadows. "Beware the ghost pirate of Whitby!"

"Who's walking down my old tunnel?" Nora croaked. "Who wants their throat cut?" She grabbed Malachy around the neck, and he pretended she was strangling him.

Soon they were all laughing, trying to scare one another. Only Lizzie remained silent as they walked deeper and deeper into the dark tunnel. There might not be ghosts, but there was definitely *something* strange about this place.

★ ★ ★

Just as Elsie had said, the tunnel's other end was right by the road. Everybody ran the rest of the way, past the gates of the Dunsley estate and onto the lawns where the circus was pitched. A stern-looking figure was waiting for them, looking at his watch — Fitzy.

"It's nice of you all to show up. Do you think this is a vacation?" he demanded.

"Sorry, Pop," Malachy said. Nobody wanted to look Fitzy in the eye.

"It just won't do. Nora, Erin, Dru: you all need to be in top form for the show," Fitzy said. "I want you to give your very best performance for the people of Whitby. That's what the Maharaja is paying to see. So get rehearsing, or so help me I'll take my whip to you!"

As the three cast members ran off to rehearse, Fitzy turned his gaze on Malachy and Lizzie. "Malachy, come with me. We need to figure out the parade route. And you, Lizzie, go and help Hari exercise the elephants now that he's decided to show his face again."

Stranger and stranger, Lizzie thought as she walked over to the tents where the animal cages were kept. So it *had* been Hari she'd seen heading out to the moors, and by the sound of it, he'd been out there all day.

"Where have you been?" Lizzie demanded when she got to the tent. "Thought you had chores?"

"I just did some exploring," Hari said with a vague wave of his hand. "You lead Akula if you like. I'll guide Sashi. We can take the others later. There's a lake down by the ice house where they can drink some water and cool off."

Be like that then, Lizzie thought. *Looks like everyone's got secrets around here.* She giggled as Akula's tickly trunk nuzzled her under the arm. "Come on then, girl. You need to stretch your legs, don't you?"

She kept a careful eye out for old Johnson as they led the two elephants down the gravel path toward the lake. If he saw that the elephants were out of their cages, he'd probably burst a blood vessel. But the gardener was nowhere to be seen.

The lake was broad and still, with a duck house on the far side and a marble statue of the Greek god Pan on a tiny island in the middle. Soon the elephants were wading gratefully into the water, splashing one another with their trunks.

"We do have permission to do this, don't we?" Lizzie asked doubtfully as they turned the huge animals loose.

"Johnson didn't say we *couldn't*," Hari said with a grin.

"Make sure the elephants don't knock the statue over then," Lizzie warned him. "Fitzy would have to pay for a new one . . ."

She checked over her shoulder one last time, but as there was no sign of the cantankerous groundskeeper, she stretched out in the grass and closed her eyes. For the first time since this morning, when she'd nearly drowned, Lizzie felt like she could relax.

Was it only last night that she and Dru had gone dancing across these lawns? She remembered the flickering candles still burning on the banquet table, the smell of the night flowers, and the gentle pressure of his arm around her waist. It was so easy to return there in her imagination. Back to the laughter and the starlight . . .

Suddenly the sound of shouting roused her from her daydream. Lizzie sat bolt upright. The elephants were still there, sloshing around in the lake, but Hari was gone. And now she heard what the angry voice was shouting:

"Thief! Don't you try to run, you little devil. I saw what you did!"

CHAPTER 11

Only a few yards away from her, Johnson, the groundskeeper, held Hari firmly by the collar and was lifting him up onto his tiptoes. Hari's face was flushed, and Lizzie knew instantly that the man was choking him.

"I'm going to send for the police," Johnson growled. "No circus for you. I can spot the likes of you a mile off."

Lizzie scrambled to her feet and ran to him. "Let him breathe! You're strangling him!"

Johnson relaxed his grip a little, but didn't let the boy go.

Hari clutched at his throat, gasping. "Lizzie . . . get Fitzy . . ."

"What are you doing to him?" Lizzie yelled. "Stop it!"

The groundskeeper blinked in surprise at Lizzie's fury. "I'm doing my job," he protested. "I found this little weasel snooping around in the gardens, up to no good."

"You're a rotten liar. You're just picking on him 'cause he's Indian!" Lizzie shouted.

Johnson's mouth opened and closed, but no sound came out of it. Lizzie thought he looked like an ugly fish.

"I reckon he's the thief who stole Lady Susannah's jewels," the groundskeeper finally managed to grunt. "And I can prove it."

"You're crazy," Hari managed to say. "You've had it in for me since we came here. Admit it."

"I saw you shovin' something black in your pocket!" Johnson shouted, shaking Hari like a terrier with a rabbit. "It was a bit of her ladyship's jet, wasn't it? You stashed it out here, didn't you?"

"No!"

"Prove it, then," Johnson said triumphantly. "Turn out your pockets."

Hari tried to wriggle free, but Johnson held his collar tightly and grabbed his arm for good measure.

"Come on, Hari," Lizzie said, giving Johnson a glare that could burn through steel. "You'd better do as he says. I know you didn't steal nothing."

"No! I won't do it!" Hari yelled. "He can't make me."

Lizzie stepped forward, wondering why Hari had said that. Surely he didn't have anything to hide.

"Oh, I can make you, all right!" Johnson set off toward the castle, hauling Hari with him. "I'll drag you in front of the Maharaja, and you can tell him why you've got your pockets full of his fiancée's jewels. Then we'll see what's what!"

Lizzie ran along behind the groundskeeper as he hauled Hari all the way to the front doors. He shoved them open with his shoulder, revealing a startled balding man in the hallway — the chief butler, Collins. Lizzie recognized him from the grand dinner.

"Fetch the Maharaja, Collins," Johnson barked. "I think he'll want to see what this little brat has been squirreling away while his back was turned."

"Right away," the butler muttered through his teeth. He gave Lizzie and Hari a distasteful look. "Perhaps the children could be taken to wait outside?"

"They won't get up to any mischief with me here to watch 'em," Johnson said, glowering.

"We're not thieves," Hari snapped at him. "You'll see."

"Not another word out of either of you, or I'll crack your heads together!" the groundskeeper snapped.

Collins rolled his eyes and disappeared up the great sweeping staircase. Lizzie stood quivering with anger at Johnson being so brutal and stupid. She was finally inside the magnificent castle, and she couldn't even enjoy it. The moment was ruined.

When Collins returned, he was alone. "The Maharaja would like you to bring the young lady and gentleman up to his study. Preferably with all their bones intact."

Hari chose that moment to wrench himself out of Johnson's grip. He grabbed Lizzie's hand, defying the gardener to lay another finger on them. "Lead on," he told Collins, with a cool confidence that made Johnson even angrier.

The staircase led up past oak-paneled galleries and across a balcony. Lizzie gasped at the luxury and opulence they were walking through. Tall paintings with gilded frames loomed over her, showing serious-faced men and women in old-fashioned clothes — she couldn't guess who they were. Fresh flowers had been arranged in huge silver vases, and a marble statue of a dancing Greek lady stood at the balcony's end.

What must it be like to pass by these wonderful things every single day, on your way down to breakfast? Lizzie wondered. Even the knives and forks here were probably made from gold and silver. She supposed the Maharaja must be used to it by now. It was what he was born to, after all.

Once they seemed to have reached the very heart of the castle, Collins opened the door onto a study lined with books. Lady Susannah was sitting on the desk — Lizzie was startled at that, as it hardly seemed very ladylike — while the Maharaja paced back and forth, admiring her from different angles.

"Exquisite," he said. "Stupendous."

"He's proud of her, isn't he?" Lizzie whispered, nudging Hari.

"It's not her he's talking about," Hari said in a grim voice. "Look at her neck."

Lizzie looked and her eyes grew wide. Sitting on Lady Susannah's perfect white throat was a deep crimson gemstone set in a golden surround.

It has to be a fake jewel, Lizzie thought. Because there was only one other thing it could be, and that would be impossible — surely it would be worth more than the entire castle and the grounds put together. Her mouth went dry at the thought, and a quiver went through her.

Johnson was about to speak, but the Maharaja interrupted. "Come in, children."

Lizzie glanced at Lady Susannah's face, hoping she was feeling well enough to have a reading from her now. She was smiling, but Lizzie could tell it was forced. *Poor thing*, she thought. *Her jet jewelry still ain't turned up, and nobody's any closer to finding it.*

Lizzie let her gaze drop to the gemstone. Beautiful wasn't the word for it. It turned sunlight into fire, glowing with vivid color. This was no fake. This was a ruby, the largest one in the country. Possibly the whole world.

"You asked me what gift I would be giving to Queen Victoria." The Maharaja had white cotton gloves on, and he held a pointing finger up to the ruby. "And now you can see it — the Heart of Durga. The world's largest ruby."

Lizzie wobbled on the spot. She drank in the glorious sight with her eyes. It was so beautiful it was making her feel light-headed.

"Do you think it is beautiful?" the Maharaja asked.

What a crazy question. As if anyone could think anything different. But the Maharaja seemed totally serious, as if he genuinely cared about Lizzie's opinion.

"Oh, yes," she agreed. "It's the loveliest thing I've ever put my eyes on."

"It is a priceless treasure of India," Hari said.

Lizzie caught her breath. She could hear cold anger in Hari's voice. The Maharaja beamed, thinking Hari was being polite, completely missing his rage.

"Priceless? You should lock it up, then!" exploded Johnson. "Especially with this little thief around."

Lady Susannah's smile vanished. "I beg your pardon?"

"I caught 'im snooping around in the gardens by himself," Johnson said. "Looking for a place to hide the jewels he stole, no doubt, so he wouldn't get caught with them."

"You think this boy stole her ladyship's jet?" The Maharaja frowned. "But where is your proof? Small boys love to explore gardens. When I was a boy, I was always climbing up trees and digging in the dirt."

"I saw him putting something in his pocket," the groundskeeper insisted. "Something black and shiny! You can't tell me that ain't Whitby jet he was squirreling away."

"I dunno what you think you saw, but Hari's no thief!" Lizzie yelled angrily. "He's my friend, and he's kind and gentle, and he's nicer than you could ever be!"

The Maharaja clapped his hands briskly. "I will have silence." It was the voice of a man who was used to being obeyed. Everyone immediately did as he commanded, even Johnson.

"Young man," the Maharaja told Hari, "please forgive the imposition, but I must ask you to turn out your pockets."

Hari shrugged. "All you had to do was ask politely." He emptied his pockets onto the Maharaja's desk, producing a fistful of peanuts, some string, a large tooth from who knew what animal, and finally a shiny black stone.

The Maharaja picked it up and turned it around with interest. His eyebrows rose as he saw the form of a snail-like creature embedded in the rock. "What a magnificent specimen. Can you tell me what it is?"

"It's an ammonite," Hari said.

The Maharaja laughed. "Fossil would have done perfectly well." His body shook as he bubbled over with laughter now. "Oh, dear, Mr. Johnson. Oh, dear me. I am afraid your sleuthing skills fall rather short of the mark."

Hands on hips, the Maharaja roared with laughter until he had to stop, lean against the desk, and wipe his eyes. "Whitby jet, indeed."

"May I have my fossil back now, please?" Hari asked.

"Since you found it on the castle grounds, it is technically *my* fossil," the Maharaja corrected, "but let's not quibble over it, shall we? Johnson, give the young lad his treasure back. And I think you owe him an apology, too."

"Sorry," grumbled Johnson, not even looking at Hari. He quickly added, "But I had your best interests at heart, Your Excellency. I've looked after these gardens for years.

You can't expect me to let young hooligans go tearin' through them any which way they please."

The Maharaja crossed the room to the window and put his hands behind his back. "You do a splendid job, Johnson. The gardens are quite magnificent . . ." His voice trailed off.

"Is something wrong?" Lady Susannah asked.

"Johnson, you might want to get back to the gardens. There appear to be a pair of elephants trampling through your geraniums."

"*Elephants!?*" Johnson jumped in the air as if he'd been jabbed in the backside. He pushed past Hari and Lizzie and ran down the hallway, nearly knocking Collins the butler off the balcony on his way.

Lizzie ran to the window to see. It was no joke. Without Hari there to watch them, the elephants had clambered out of the pond and were lumbering in a straight line toward their enclosure, plowing through everything in their path.

Johnson's despairing cry drifted up the stairs. Moments later, they saw him running out across the lawn, flailing his arms wildly.

"Hmm," said the Maharaja. "Elephants don't appreciate being shouted at. Despite his temper, Johnson is a good gardener. I would hate for him to be trampled flat on his own lawn. You two had better go and round them up."

"Right you are, Your Excellency," Lizzie said, dropping into a curtsey.

"I can't wait for the parade this evening," the Maharaja said with a giggle. He was still as full of joy as any child would be. "In fact, watching those elephants roaming about has given me a great idea . . ."

"Dare I ask?" said Lady Susannah, raising an eyebrow.

The Maharaja leaned close and whispered something in her ear. Lady Susannah's eyes widened in surprise and she giggled.

Lizzie took that as her cue to leave.

Soon after, she and Hari were leading two happy elephants back to their pens. Fitzy, to Lizzie's relief, took their side. If Johnson was dumb enough to drag the animal handler off and leave the elephants unsupervised, what did he expect to happen? Besides, the Maharaja had been very understanding, so no more needed to be said about it.

"He's such a nice man," Lizzie said to Hari.

"Who? Fitzy?"

"No, the Maharaja. He's the sweetest rich guy I ever met."

"Sweet?" Hari scowled. "He's no better than a thief. How dare he steal that ruby from India and give it to Queen Victoria, as if it was his to give away? And he has the gall to fret when someone steals from him!"

Suddenly, Lizzie wondered if it *was* Hari who had stolen the jet jewelry. To her, the jet had seemed like it was worth a fortune, but that was before she'd seen the Heart of Durga. To someone whose country had lost such a treasure, surely stealing one necklace in revenge was a mere drop in the ocean . . .

CHAPTER 12

Making things with her hands always made Lizzie
feel better. Back in the days when she lived in Rat's Castle,
she'd made paper flowers from colored streamers to sell
on the street. She was as quick and neat as any seamstress,
with nimble fingers that would have made her an excellent
pickpocket if her life had taken a different direction.

Thankfully, Fitzy's circus had saved her from all that.

Now Lizzie sat in her wagon and threaded the
shells she'd collected onto black cord. With a tool she'd
borrowed from one of the handymen, she'd made holes
in them so the cockleshells would lie flat. Two identical
bracelets steadily took shape.

"My bonnie lies over the ocean," she sang as she
worked. "My bonnie lies over the sea . . ."

Erin and Nora would love their bracelets, she knew.
Maybe, if she had a few rich clients come for readings,
she'd be able to buy a couple of beads of real Whitby jet
and add them as spacers between the bigger shells. It might
not be a whole jet necklace, but it ought to make Nora
happy.

For all you know, Nora's got Lady Susannah's necklace stashed somewhere, a nasty voice whispered in the back of her mind. *Maybe Nora and Hari stole it together . . .*

Lizzie chatted nervously to herself to keep the suspicious thoughts away. "'She sells seashells on the seashore.' Well, that's dumb, isn't it? Who's going to buy seashells on the seashore? There's loads of 'em lying around. Foolish girl."

She was proudly laying out the finished bracelets on her dressing table when the distant boom of a gong rang out from the show tent.

"That's the parade getting ready to start!" Lizzie said in a panic. "Where'd the time go?"

She hurried out of her wagon and set off at a run toward the show tent, where lines of circus folk were already forming. Then, thinking again, she changed direction and ran to the tea tent. The parade would take hours, and she hadn't eaten all day.

The tea-tent door flaps were usually tied open, but now they were hanging down, blocking her path. *Surely, Ma Sullivan didn't close up shop already?* Lizzie thought as she wrestled her way through.

But Ma Sullivan was there, and so were Nora and Erin, all bending over something. The twins bounced up like jackrabbits, grinning widely, while Ma Sullivan rummaged around behind the counter. Lizzie saw she was shoving something out of sight.

"Hello, Lizzie me love," Ma Sullivan said, standing up and wiping her brow. All three of them were grinning like toy monkeys. "Here for a quick bowl of stew before we leave?"

"Yes, please," Lizzie said, eyeing them suspiciously.

Nora and Erin watched her take her seat. Neither spoke. Lizzie's thoughts were racing now. What could possibly be going on? All the Sullivans seemed to be acting shifty. There was one explanation, and she didn't want to dwell on it, but she couldn't help it. It came back to her, just like it had in her wagon.

She'd seen Nora fastening a jet necklace around her neck. Her visions were *never* wrong. Whether she'd stolen the necklace herself or not, it seemed she must have it now. And who could Nora trust not to betray her, out of the whole circus? Her mother and sister, of course.

Were Ma Sullivan and Erin in on it, too? Lizzie wondered. She banished the thought as a smiling Ma Sullivan served her up a brimming bowl of stew and a big piece of bread to sop it up with.

"Get that down you, dear," she said. "But don't bolt it now. You've a good quarter hour before the parade sets off and I don't want you getting indigestion."

Lizzie dug in, though she wasn't feeling very hungry now. Her stomach squirmed like a live oyster being doused in lemon juice. Lately, it seemed her visions were bringing her more pain than joy. If she hadn't seen Nora putting that necklace on, she'd still be happy and trusting, with no idea anything might be wrong. Now she had no choice but to be suspicious of the friends who had become like sisters to her.

And she hated it.

* * *

The parade was nearly ready to set off for town. Fitzy, wearing a red spangled jacket and brandishing a golden baton, strode up and down inspecting the circus performers who were lined up on the castle courtyard. From the silk-draped elephants in front to the trapeze artists in spangles at the back, everyone was wearing their very best costumes. They all held handfuls of fliers ready to be thrown out to the public.

Lizzie grinned to see all her friends in the procession. There was the band in the middle, ready to march. The clowns were going through their warm-up exercises, doing jumping jacks and push-ups in full makeup. Leo, the circus lion, paced back and forth in his cage. All the Sullivan boys were astride their ponies, looking more handsome than ever in their Wild West gear. Erin and Nora had quickly changed into their elegant bareback ballet dresses. Everywhere Lizzie looked, colors shone out more brightly than Johnson's flowers — scarlet and gold, silver-blue, and rich green.

Then, without warning, the castle doors boomed open, and a figure came striding out, every bit as colorful as the parade. It was the Maharaja, wearing a traditional silk outfit and a splendid turban. Lizzie felt a jolt of excitement when she saw the Heart of Durga gleaming from the turban's front.

"Look at you all!" cried the Maharaja. "You are magnificent! Oh, happy day when I invited you to visit us in Whitby."

"The honor is all ours," Fitzy said with a polite bow. "I take it you'll be watching the parade with the Mayor and his wife?"

"Watch it?" the Maharaja said in horror. "My dear man, I wish to be *in* the parade!"

Fitzy coughed into his fist. "Naturally. Perhaps you would like to lead it alongside me?"

"I shall ride on one of the elephants," Gurinder Bhatti announced. "That one." He pointed at Akula.

Hari held the elephant's guiding rope and glanced up at his uncle. "I'm afraid that would not be a good idea," Zezete said smoothly. "The elephants do not know you, sir. A parade can be a noisy business, and they need to know their rider for such an occasion. Their trust has to be earned."

"Pah," the Maharaja scoffed. "I have ridden elephants countless times. Probably more than you, in fact. There's nothing to it." He walked to Akula's side and tugged on the ropes holding her howdah secure. Lizzie remembered that word from when Hari had first helped her climb aboard Akula — a howdah was a sort of padded seat that perched on an elephant's back.

Fitzy tried to protest, but the Maharaja waved him away. "I insist. Please don't fuss. I do know what I'm doing."

He was going to get his own way, Lizzie knew. For some reason, that made her feel nervous. She didn't like the way Zezete and Hari were glaring at the Maharaja, and she knew that the elephants got upset when people argued and shouted. Like many animals, they could pick up on a mood, and it could make them touchy.

Then, sudden as a bullet through her head, it hit — a vision. Lizzie clenched her eyes shut and stood with her fists balled, shaking as if she were having a fit.

She saw the Maharaja riding on top of an elephant, smiling and waving. The girl leading the elephant through the crowded Whitby streets was Lizzie herself! The next moment, the elephant trumpeted and reared up. Screams rang out and people began to panic.

"Don't!" Lizzie suddenly cried out at the top of her voice.

The Maharaja was already perched on Akula's back. Silence fell. Everyone stared at Lizzie. She stood, shaking and breathless, the center of attention.

"I beg your pardon?" the Maharaja said.

"Don't ride on Akula," Lizzie begged. But even as she spoke, she struggled to find the right words. How could she possibly convince him? If she said she'd had a vision, he'd probably laugh in her face. A superstitious local girl like Elsie might take her visions seriously, but surely not someone as rich and powerful as Gurinder Bhatti.

"It's . . . it's such a long way down," Lizzie began. "What if you fell off? What if Akula threw you? You could be hurt terribly."

The Maharaja wasn't angry. "Dear girl, you do not know elephants as I do. This elephant is as gentle as any lamb."

Hari shrugged and offered Lizzie Akula's guiding rope. "Want to lead her?" he said quietly, so nobody else could hear. "She trusts you."

Lizzie thought quickly. *If I'm not leading her, then the vision can't come true! All I have to do is lead a different elephant, and the Maharaja will be safe!*

"No, you take Akula," she said. "She loves you more than any of us. I'll lead Sashi."

Hari looked at her oddly. "Suit yourself," he said, shaking his head.

Lizzie smiled, feeling clever that she'd thought of a way to avert disaster as the procession began to move off.

* * *

The plan was for the parade to head along the coast road, down the zigzag pathways into town, and across the swing bridge over the Esk River. The acrobats and jugglers would put on a little show, then everyone would troop back across the bridge and up the coast toward Dunsley Castle again.

Lizzie led Sashi the elephant toward the end of the bridge, where a huge crowd had gathered. "Great idea to cross the river," Malachy said, keeping pace with her. "Nice and high up, no buildings in the way to block the view. They'll be able to see us for miles around."

"This bridge will take an elephant's weight, won't it?" Lizzie wondered.

"We'll soon find out," Malachy said, grinning. He jumped up and down on the spot. "Seems sturdy enough to me."

"Here they come!" Lizzie heard a child shout.

The crowds pointed and chatted excitedly as they heard the blast of trumpets and the booming of a big bass drum. The parade rounded the curve of the street with the Maharaja, riding on Akula and waving, at the front of the pack. By the look of it, the whole town had turned out to see them. Children rode on shoulders, and fishermen stood on the decks of their boats.

"There's Elsie!" Lizzie exclaimed, waving frantically. The fishergirl was watching with her entire family from their little boat. She caught Lizzie's eye and waved back.

"And there's Lady Susannah," Malachy said. Fan in hand, the lady was watching the parade from the near end of the bridge, where some other important-looking people were standing. "Shame there's no royal box, huh?"

"There's the Mayor and Mayoress, too," Lizzie added. "Look at his big gold chain. It don't look like much next to the Maharaja's ruby, though, does it? And there's . . . *Billy?*"

Lizzie stared as the seaside con man came sidling up to the group of wealthy people. *He must be getting ready to pick a pocket*, she thought. And he'd probably be successful, too, since everyone was busy watching the circus parade and acting as if he wasn't there. Rich people always did that, Lizzie knew — anything common or vulgar, they just pretended they couldn't see it.

Now Billy was moving in on Lady Susannah. Lizzie stiffened to see him strut up to her like that, his hands in his pockets, as if he were the king of the whole town.

Her ladyship produced her big black feathery fan and held it in front of her face like a barrier. It didn't stop Billy. He leaned in and began to whisper in her ear. There was something sickening about his oily grin. Lady Susannah looked trapped, fluttering her fan nervously.

"Malachy, look!"

"I see him. What a rude man. We can't let that weasel mess about with the Maharaja's lady friend!"

As they approached the group of dignitaries, Lizzie bellowed, "Hey! Leave the lady alone!"

Billy jumped, as if he'd been caught robbing a safe. Lady Susannah was startled, but looked grateful to see them and gave the children a smile and a little wave.

"I don't think the lady appreciates your attention," Malachy yelled to Billy.

"Get out of here!" Lizzie snapped at him, jerking her thumb.

Billy shrugged. "Can't blame me for trying," he called, giving them a wink. Whistling a jaunty tune, he slipped off into the crowd without a backward glance.

Lady Susannah's cheeks were flushed as she fanned herself. "You are heroes, the pair of you!" she called to Lizzie and Malachy. "Thank you for rescuing me from that dreadful man."

By now, the front of the parade was moving out over the bridge. Lizzie watched nervously as the two elephants lumbered through the crowd. The Maharaja was busy flinging fliers like confetti to the left and right. "Roll up, roll up!" he shouted. "Spectacular circus tomorrow night! Bring the family!"

"He looks like he's wanted to do this all his life," Lizzie said to Malachy.

In the midst of the noise and chaos, Hari beckoned Lizzie over. She gave Malachy Sashi's rope to hold and walked to the head of the procession.

"I need a favor," he muttered. "Take Akula's rope and lead her for a moment, would you? I'll be right back."

"What?" Lizzie said. "Why?" Cold panic took hold of her. If she was leading Akula, then the vision could come true after all. "I can't!"

"It's only for a moment," Hari insisted. "I have a quick errand I need to run in town. Please, Lizzie? It's really important, and I might not get another chance."

Lizzie reluctantly took Akula's rope. "You'd better come right back," she warned.

Hari ran off immediately. He weaved in and out of the bystanders, moving toward the rows of shops beyond the harbor.

"Some errand," Lizzie muttered to herself. "Looks more like a shopping trip to me." She walked at the very front of the procession, leading Akula and feeling more and more nervous. At least the elephant was peaceful and content. Lizzie stroked her cheek as they walked. "Good girl," she whispered.

The Maharaja, high above, waved wildly to the crowd. "Ladies and gentlemen! Come one, come all, to Fitzy's Circus of Wonders and Marvels!"

Just then, a harsh voice from the crowd yelled out, "Go home! You don't belong here!"

Lizzie glanced around to see who had spoken, but there were so many people it was impossible to tell. Then, from out of the crowd, a rock came hurtling through the air, arching over the tops of people's heads. It struck Akula's side with a thud.

Lizzie screamed and Akula trumpeted in pain. The elephant flung her head to the left and right, and Lizzie fought to hold onto her rope, but it was no use. Her vision was coming true, and there was nothing she could do to stop it.

More screams rang out from the crowd, and people ran for cover as the maddened elephant reared up . . .

CHAPTER 13

The elephant trumpeted and raged like something from an ancient battle. One man dived over the side of the bridge and fell into the river as Akula's head swung toward him. The crowd up ahead screamed and ran, cramming against one another in their haste to get out of the way.

"It's going to charge!" someone screamed. "We'll all be killed!"

Akula's front legs came down on the bridge. Lizzie felt the whole thing shiver under her feet, and that sent a fresh wave of panic through the crowd. Malachy had been sure the bridge would take an elephant's weight, but a panicked elephant?

Sashi stood still, twitching his trunk nervously as Akula reared up again, her legs waving. The Maharaja clung on, one hand clutching the howdah straps and the other pressed to his head. *Of course*, Lizzie thought. *He's scared the turban with the ruby in it will fall off.*

"She ain't going to charge!" Lizzie yelled. She still had hold of the rope, which tugged and strained in her grip as Akula thrashed about. "She's gentle, she just had a fright."

Nobody listened. Nobody even seemed to hear her. Lizzie stood her ground as screaming people ran past her. The end of the bridge was bottlenecked with the escaping crowd now, pressed so tightly together they were crushing one another. People were running up to see what was happening and getting in the way of the ones who were trying to leave. It was total chaos.

There was a bloody mark on Akula's side where the rock had hit her. The crowd was making it worse, Lizzie knew. The poor elephant was panicking, feeling trapped and threatened.

In that moment, Lizzie knew Akula *would* charge if she had to. She didn't know any better. She needed to feel safe, and would plow through a crowd to get away if that was what it took.

"I've got to do something," she gasped. Zezete was further down at the other end of the bridge with the lion. He was running up to help, pushing his way through the crowd, but couldn't possibly reach them in time. Hari had run off heaven only knew where. She had to try.

Lizzie reached for Akula's trunk. The elephant's massive feet came down almost on top of her, but she forced herself to stand still and to sing. She tried to sound like Hari, with lots of up-and-down notes. She didn't know the words to his Indian songs, so she just threw in words she did know instead. *"My bonnie lies over the oo-ooo-ooocean, my bonnie lies over the see-eee-ea . . ."*

Akula hesitated and swung her great barrel-like head down. Very gently, Lizzie reached up and stroked her trunk, and when the elephant didn't flinch away, she stroked it again.

"Oh bring back my bonnie to meeee," Lizzie sang softly. "And bring a great big bag of peanuts for the best elephant in the world."

Without being asked, Akula knelt down. The look in her eye seemed to say sorry. The crowds began to settle down, murmuring, as they saw what was going on.

"Why, it's all a trick!" one man yelled angrily. "Part of the show. That girl was in control of the beast all the time."

"Nothing but a cheap stunt," someone else sneered.

Down below, in the river, the man who had dived in was hauling himself onto the shore. He wrung out his cloth cap, shrugged, and put it back on his head.

"Lizzie, what's going on?" Hari came running back, dodging in and out of the people milling aimlessly on the bridge. He was shoving a package into his pocket, wrapped in brown paper. "I heard Akula trumpeting. Is she okay?"

"She's fine *now*, no thanks to you!" Lizzie angrily handed him the guiding rope. "I hope your 'errand' was important. Someone could have been killed!"

"Akula would never hurt anyone."

"Not on purpose," Lizzie agreed. "But someone threw a rock at her, didn't they? She nearly threw the Maharaja off her back." She turned to him. "Are you all right up there, sir?"

The Maharaja waved away her concerns. "I am quite well," he said, though his hands were shaking and his turban was crooked.

"You'd better get down and walk the rest of the way," Hari suggested.

"Out of the question," the Maharaja replied. "I began this parade on an elephant, and I shall finish it on an elephant. If anyone has anything to say to me, they can say it to my face!"

As the parade began to move off again, through a muttering and agitated crowd, Lizzie found she admired the man's pride. He might be silly in some ways, but he was also brave. For all he knew, someone was still out there getting ready to throw another rock.

Lizzie wondered who had thrown the first one. She looked over the faces of the crowd, trying to spot anyone who looked angry or hateful. Then she glanced at Hari walking by her side, and another unwelcome possibility came to mind.

It could have been Hari, she thought. *He's no friend of the Maharaja's, is he? Hasn't he said, again and again, what a thief and a traitor he thinks he is? And wasn't it convenient that Hari had to rush off on an "errand," just before the rock was thrown?*

"Shut up," Lizzie whispered to her own suspicious thoughts.

It could have been him, her mind insisted. *You can't prove it wasn't.*

"Yes, I can," Lizzie told herself triumphantly. "It don't matter how much Hari hates the Maharaja. He'd never, ever hurt Akula just to put him in danger. He loves that elephant."

Malachy frowned and glanced her way. "Who are you muttering to over there?"

"Just talking to myself," Lizzie said with a sigh. "First sign of madness. Ain't that what they say?"

* * *

The setting sun was turning the waves red by the time Lizzie, Erin, and Nora finally returned to the castle grounds.

"That could have gone a lot worse," Lizzie said. "Akula calmed down pretty quick, and the crowd liked the jugglers. And when Sardini did his fire-eating, they thought it were the devil himself!"

"Do you reckon we'll get a big turnout tomorrow?" Erin asked around a huge yawn.

"If we don't, it's their loss," Nora replied. "The show's free, so people have nothing to lose by coming along."

"We'll give 'em the best show we can, and if they don't like it, they can go jump off a cliff," Erin said.

"Exactly," Lizzie said with a grin.

"The sideshows and penny gaffs had better get them properly warmed up!" Nora said, stretching. "That means you, Lizzie. Send them into the show tent with their eyes good and wide."

Lizzie reached her wagon and held the door open. "Right. Cocoa and gossip time, girls. You two fetch the drinks, and I'll get the candles lit and fluff the cushions up."

"Ah, not tonight, okay?" Erin yawned again. "Me arms and legs are dropping off, I'm that tired."

Lizzie couldn't believe what she was hearing. Cocoa and gossip was a nightly ritual. They *always* got together in Old Esther for a before-bedtime chat about boys and future plans and the dreams they all had.

"Me, too," said Nora. "Big day tomorrow. We should make it an early night. Lots of rest. Sleep well, Lizzie, see ya in the morning."

Lizzie felt like her world had been shaken to the foundations. One twin snubbing their get-together was bad enough, but *both*?

"Well, don't let me keep you up or nothing," Lizzie said, turning her back on them. She shut the wagon door with a bang. Then she sat on the bed, her head in her hands, and tried not to cry.

Lizzie felt something lumpy underneath her. She pulled out the shell bracelets she'd made, hidden under the quilt so Erin and Nora wouldn't see them when they came over.

"Needn't have bothered," she sniffed. She flung them under the bed, threw herself onto the pillow, and shut her eyes to the world. If everyone else was having an early night, she'd have one, too.

* * *

The day of the gala performance dawned, and Lizzie woke from blessedly dreamless sleep.

Preparations were already in full swing. Like a clockwork machine with all its parts in good order, the circus went to work. Everyone had to keep up the pace; there was no time for any one member to fret or lag behind. Rehearsals that had filled the days before were given a final polish. Costumes were checked for any stray threads or last-minute mending. Lions, elephants, and camels were groomed until they seemed as bright and new as the figures on a Noah's Ark toy.

Finally, with an hour left to go, Fitzy gathered everyone on the castle lawn. Excitement seethed in the crowd. The circus folk couldn't wait to get started, and Fitzy knew it. Lizzie grinned at him as he made his way up to his soapbox.

"Look at you all, fizzing like the bubbles in a bottle of champagne," Fitzy said with a happy laugh. "Let's give the bottle an extra shake or two before we pop the cork, shall we?"

The circus folk laughed and cheered. Fitzy lifted his hat to them. "When I was just a little boy, playing at circuses under the table, I promised myself one day I'd put on a show for the King himself," he continued. "Well, this is the next best thing, folks. The Maharaja Gurinder Bhatti — Queen Victoria's friend! Maybe this time next year we'll be at her home, Buckingham Palace!"

In that moment, Lizzie could believe it. She wondered if she'd get to do a reading for the Queen. Maybe she could speak to her dead husband, Albert, and comfort her in her hour of grief . . .

"But among all these la-di-dah high society types, my dears," Fitzy went on, "I want you to remember why we're in this business in the first place. It doesn't matter how many kings and queens you have in your audience. What matters is this: you have the power to make every single person watching *feel* like a king or queen. That's a rare and precious thing. I want to see royal smiles everywhere I look, is that understood? Work your magic today, ladies and gents. Make me proud."

The crowd cheered, then broke up, bubbling over with excitement. Lizzie ran across the lawn to her wagon as if she were running across the clouds in the sky.

It was circus custom to open the sideshows and penny gaffs some hours before the main performance. They helped to warm the crowd up and bring in some extra money on top of ticket sales. That was where Lizzie's job came in. Of course, no one would be paying her today. The Maharaja had already agreed to a handsome fee with Fitzy for the whole setup — for the people of Whitby, the whole show was free, sideshows and all.

Lizzie changed into her scarlet and gold clairvoyant's robes, which were long and baggy so she could pull them on over the top of her regular clothes if she had to. Ma Sullivan had sewn them for her after the old ones her predecessor, Madame Aurora, had worn had finally become too threadbare for use. A gauzy veil over her face completed the ensemble.

The fortune-telling tent stood by the main entrance to the castle grounds, with Lizzie's hand-painted wooden sign propped outside. *The Magnificent Lizzie Brown*, it declared. *Genuine Clairvoyant — Thousands of Testimonials — Eighth Wonder of the World*. Lizzie wasn't quite sure what the other seven wonders of the world were supposed to be, but thought Akula was probably one of them.

Inside, the tent was cozy and a bit stuffy. All her props were in a wicker case where the circus porters had left them for her. One by one, she took them out and put them in place: velvet cloth on the round table, crystal ball and incense burner on the side table, Tarot cards spread out in a fan shape, a little ivory statue of a fat Chinese man next to them.

Lizzie loved setting up her tent. It had become a little ritual to her, a way of feeling at home in a new city or campsite. The last thing to do was light the incense. Curling gray tongues of sandalwood smoke wafted into the darkened air.

It wasn't that these props heightened her psychic abilities, but her customers expected a mystical atmosphere, so she gave it to them. Once everything was ready, Lizzie sat back, smiling behind her veil, and waited for the first customer to appear.

Sure enough, one did. A curly head popped around the tent door. "Y'all right, Liz? It's me, Elsie. Is it you under all that getup?"

"Come in," Lizzie said, "and let the tent flap down behind you. You said you wanted to know something for sure?"

Elsie shivered as she sat down. "It's the ghost ship," she whispered. "I couldn't say before, because I didn't know if I could trust you. But . . . I think I know who it is."

Lizzie's mind flashed back to the hooded figure looming over the bright green light, with fog billowing all around it.

"I think it's my brother," Elsie said.

Lizzie frowned. "What, playing tricks or something?"

"My *dead* brother."

Suddenly Lizzie understood what she meant. Of course — this was a fishing town, and tragedies at sea surely happened all the time. "When did he . . . pass away?"

"Three years ago. He was lost at sea. They never found a trace of him, nor of his ship, the *Green Linnet*. Jack Hodgkins and Selwyn Booth, his friends, they was lost, too."

"I'm sorry," Lizzie said. But Elsie's eyes were dry. Lizzie got the feeling Elsie had already shed all the tears she would cry for her brother long ago. The people up here weren't soft.

"Can you talk to him? If he's not at rest — if it's *him* haunting Whitby harbor and keeping me awake at night — then I want to know why."

Unfinished business, Lizzie thought to herself. Ghosts who still had something left to do on earth couldn't cross over to the afterlife. "I can talk to the dead, if they're willing," she said. "But I need something to make a connection. Do you have anything that belonged to him?"

Elsie set a clay pipe on the table between them. It was still stuffed with old, unsmoked tobacco. "I used to fill it for him every night, so he could have his smoke when he came in from sea," Elsie said, her voice catching a little. "Didn't have the heart to throw it away, did I?"

"Just as well that you didn't," Lizzie said. She held the pipe — still warm from Elsie's body — in her cupped hands and closed her eyes.

Instantly she was somewhere else. Bright sunshine in a clear blue sky and waves dancing below her feet — she was hovering, weightless, out on the open sea.

A woman wearing a dress made from shiny scales and with seaweed twisted through her long, greenish hair, rose up from the sea. "Why are you here?" she asked. "Who do you seek, child who walks between the worlds?"

"I'm looking for Elsie's brother," Lizzie told it.

The figure shook her head. "Matt Towersey is not here, child. Nor is Jack Hodgkins, nor Selwyn Booth. Gone from the world of men are they. They sing and laugh together in Fiddler's Green."

With a gasp, Lizzie was suddenly back in her tent. She could still see the after-image of the ethereal figure behind her eyes.

"What did you see?" Elsie demanded, her voice rising. "The ghost — is it him?"

"I . . . I spoke to someone," Lizzie said, feeling shaken. "It was some sort of an ocean spirit, I think. A kindly one. It said Matt Towersey was in Fiddler's Green."

When she heard those words, Elsie clapped her hands to her cheeks, and the tears began to flow in earnest. "I never told you his name!" she said. "You are a real psychic after all!"

"I don't think your brother's the ghost on the ship," Lizzie said carefully.

"He's not." Elsie was certain now. "Not if he's in Fiddler's Green. He always used to joke about that lovely place . . . you've never heard of it, have you?"

"No. Sorry."

Elsie wiped her eyes. "It's the sailors' paradise. Bad sailors go down to Davy Jones's Locker, but the good ones go to Fiddler's Green until they're ready to go to heaven. The stories say you see your old friends there, and the ale never runs dry."

"So his soul's at peace."

"Yes, and thank god for that." Elsie stood up, looking worried. "It's my own soul I've got to worry about now."

"What do you mean?" Lizzie couldn't understand why the girl wasn't more cheerful. She thought she'd given her *good* news.

"That ghost ship's still out there, in't it? If it's not my brother's ghost, then whose is it?"

* * *

For the next two hours, Lizzie read palms and answered questions. Her tent was never empty. All the girls wanted to know if their sweethearts would come back to them, and all the boys wanted to know if they would be rich . . . it was the same old story, just with different names and faces.

Lizzie was getting better at telling people the truth without upsetting them, though. All you had to do was focus on the good things you saw. There was always something if you looked hard enough — even if it was just the chance to turn aside bad luck before it happened.

Just then the tent flap opened again, and Lizzie sat up, startled, as Lady Susannah entered her tent. The lady sat down opposite her and gave a tight smile. Out came the fan, wafting away the incense smoke.

"Sorry," Lizzie said. "It's a bit thick, I know."

"I don't usually believe in this sort of thing," the lady said, her voice a low murmur. "But I have watched person after person come out of this tent singing your praises. So I am willing to try."

"You want to know about your jewelry?" Excitement seized Lizzie. Finally, a chance to find out the truth and put suspicion to rest!

"Ha! Oh, no. This is something far more important."

Lizzie opened her mouth and shut it again. "You'd better give me your hand, then. The left one."

"Wait. I want you to swear, on your mother's grave, that you'll never tell anyone what you see. Not a soul, you understand?"

"I promise," Lizzie whispered. She had the feeling of being on the edge of a cliff again. Only the slightest push, and she would go over . . .

Lady Susannah licked her lips and took Lizzie's hands in a tight grip. Her fingers were cold and smooth. "Tell me whether my Maharaja will marry me."

"Ohhh," Lizzie said. "Now I understand." Lady Susannah, for all her finery and fancy manners, was no different from the fishing girls from the village.

The lady frowned, then broke into a wide smile. "Yes. Clever girl. I am quite head over heels in love, and I am *desperate* to marry him. But he's not asked me yet, and I fear he never will. Is that silly of me?"

"'Course it's not!" *Just another girl with a sweetheart problem*, Lizzie thought. "Let's be having your hand, then. Er . . . my lady."

Lizzie stroked her finger down Lady Susannah's line of life. Images began to appear, as they always did. She saw a happy little blond girl riding on a pony while a second sour-faced girl, blond like the first, jealously watched.

When Lizzie described the image, Lady Susannah nodded eagerly. "Jennifer Meadows always hated me," she smirked. "I showed her, though. Now hurry up and show me the future."

More childhood scenes followed: a party, a girl running in tears from a clown, a kitten with a ribbon around its neck. As she saw the scenes, Lizzie described to Lady Susannah what she was seeing. Then, without warning, a horrible scene appeared:

Lady Susannah was a young woman now, staring up in terror as above her loomed a swarthy man in a long robe, holding a huge curved sword.

He laughed, as if he relished her fear. "Time to die, my pretty!"

Then there was a bright flash, Lady Susannah screamed, and the sword came plunging down . . .

CHAPTER 14

"What?" Lady Susannah demanded. "What is it? What did you see?"

"Someone tried to kill you!" Lizzie said, horrified. "A man with a big sharp sword. He was standing over you and laughing. How did you escape? Did the police catch him?"

This wasn't filling in missing pieces of the puzzle — this was just making the puzzle even more baffling. Who would want to kill Lady Susannah? Lizzie could understand stealing from her — the jet was worth a fortune — but murder? Possibilities raced through her mind. Maybe the Maharaja had enemies who would never let him marry an Englishwoman. Or maybe a group of assassins had come over from India, wanting revenge on him and his family?

Lady Susannah snatched her hand away. "Those unpleasant incidents are in the *past*," she said, as if Lizzie had done something stupid. "I believe I asked you to tell me about my future?"

"Sorry," Lizzie mumbled. "I'll do my best." She took Lady Susannah's hand again. Right away, a vision stood out in her mind. It was bright and perfectly clear, which told

Lizzie it was the future she was seeing. But the vision was even worse than the last.

"Do you see my wedding day?" Lady Susannah asked eagerly. "What time of year is it? Are there leaves on the trees? Hurry up, I want to know."

But what Lizzie saw was no wedding. *Lady Susannah, her hair in disarray, was wearing a dirty, ripped gray dress, and her hands were bound behind her back. She was weeping and struggling to escape from her bonds. "Please don't kill me," she pleaded to her unseen captor.*

"Someone's going to try to murder you," Lizzie gasped, dropping Lady Susannah's hand.

"Didn't I tell you not to look at the past?"

"It's not the past! You were all dirty and ragged. I saw your hands — there wasn't a wedding ring on your finger. You're not going to get married, you're going to get killed!"

"Oh, for heaven's sake." Lady Susannah slammed her hand down on the table, rattling the crystal balls. "Do I look like a schoolgirl? You and your little friends may enjoy titillating one another with tales of blood and gore, but the rest of us have outgrown such stuff. What a cruel, juvenile prank!"

"But that's what I saw! I'm sorry, but he ain't never going to marry you, and —"

"Adamant, are we? Very well. I see I shall have to have words with your employer about this." Lady Susannah stormed out of the tent, leaving Lizzie with the mental image of her weeping and struggling.

"But your life's in danger, yer ladyship!" Lizzie protested.

It was no good. Lady Susannah was already gone — and by the look of it, any customers who were still waiting had taken off, too. Of course; they wouldn't want to risk having a reading with the Magnificent Lizzie Brown if Lady Susannah didn't approve.

Lizzie sat, her stomach churning with nerves, and wondered what she should do. Clearly, some danger from the past had returned to stalk Lady Susannah in the present. Someone, possibly the same person who wanted to hurt the Maharaja, meant to kill her. And that person would strike soon.

The more she thought about it, the more Lizzie realized she hadn't broken the news to Lady Susannah very politely. "'You were all dirty and ragged,'" she muttered to herself. "Just the sort of thing a lady wants to hear. Ugh." Perhaps she should have just said her life was in danger and then added the details if she'd been pressed for them.

I should apologize, Lizzie realized. She rushed out into the crowd, trying to see where Lady Susannah had gone, but there was no sign of her.

She knocked on the Sullivans' wagon door. It was a little ajar, so she opened it the rest of the way and popped her head around. "Almost showtime!"

The girls were sprawled on the floor. Lizzie saw the wagon's storage box was open, and the sewing kit was out. Before she could see what they'd been working on, Erin slammed the box's lid down. "Don't you have customers waiting?" she said in surprise.

"All done. I'm free as a bird."

Lizzie looked at the twins, and the twins looked at Lizzie. For a moment, no one spoke.

"All right, then," Lizzie finally said. "Own up. What are you making in here? And don't say 'nothing,' because I saw you!"

Nora and Erin exchanged glances. "You mustn't tell, okay?" Nora said.

"Cross me heart."

"We're sewing new costumes," Nora whispered. "But we've got a custom in the family. A bit like wedding dresses, you know? *You can't see them until they're finished.* Nobody can. Otherwise . . ."

"Otherwise it's bad luck, and the costume's ruined, and you can't ever wear it, and you have to burn it on a big fire," Erin finished in a rush.

Lizzie shrugged. "Could have just said so in the first place. Dunno why you and your ma had to be so secretive."

"Ah, well, families, y'know?" Erin said, grinning weakly. "Hey! Speaking of our ma, you'll never guess what we found at the bottom of the storage box."

Nora produced a huge book with bits of paper poking out from between the leaves. "It's her old scrapbook!" she exclaimed.

"This goes back to before any of us were born," Erin said proudly. "Ma traveled with lots of circuses before Fitzy's. She kept souvenirs from all of them."

The book was crammed with old advertisements and folded posters, the colors still bright. In between, newspaper clippings had been pasted. Lizzie sat with the book on her lap and leafed through it eagerly. Nora and Erin sat on either side, pointing at the headlines and the pictures.

"That's Princess Caraboo!" Erin said. "She was one of Ma's friends. She wasn't really a foreign princess, she was a servant girl, but she fooled all the rich people."

"Look at these people!" Lizzie exclaimed. "Samson, the world's strongest man. Thundering Cloud, the Indian chief, and his Tomahawks of Peril. Mister Marvel, the conjuror king, assisted by the mysterious Scheherazade. Here he is again — Mister Marvel, the Modern Merlin."

The engraving showed a man with a long moustache and ponytail wearing a Chinese silk hat. He held a dove perched on his outstretched finger, as if he'd just produced it from thin air. "The mysterious Scheherazade" looked on in a spangled mask, holding up her hands in what Lizzie thought was meant to be astonishment.

"Was he really Chinese?" Lizzie wondered.

Nora laughed. "Of course not. It was all just an act. Ma said he was a handsome young man under the makeup, though."

"There's Ma!" Erin pointed at an engraving of a young woman in a fringed buckskin jacket, firing pistols from the back of a pony. "'Desperate Deborah of Dublin, the Irish Hell-Cat!'"

"Wow," Lizzie said, impressed.

"Pa always said she was a wild one," Nora said with a wide, cheeky grin. "Bet you never knew she was *that* wild, huh?"

* * *

As she headed back to her wagon, Lizzie caught sight of Lady Susannah striding angrily toward her with Fitzy in tow. Lizzie sighed. There was no chance of ducking away and hiding. She'd been seen.

"There she is!" Lady Susannah marched up and jabbed a finger in Lizzie's direction. "I warned you I'd speak to your employer, girl, and that was no idle threat!"

Lizzie braced herself. She knew she ought to apologize, but she hated the thought of saying sorry when she'd done nothing wrong.

"Lizzie, we need to sort this out," Fitzy said as Lady Susannah folded her arms and glared. "Her ladyship is quite upset."

147

"You should have heard her," the lady said. "Making up the most outrageous stories just to see the frightened look on my face. I don't call that harmless entertainment, do you?"

"Well, Lizzie? What's your side of the story?"

"I weren't trying to scare her, I promise!" Lizzie protested. "I saw danger in her future, and I was trying to *warn* her."

"I see." Fitzy tapped the side of his nose, thinking. "I'm sure you meant well, but you can understand why she'd be upset, can't you?"

"I s'pose," Lizzie admitted. Lady Susannah's stubborn refusal to take her seriously was giving her a headache. It wasn't Lizzie's fault if the warning scared her. The silly woman's life was being threatened. What was Lizzie supposed to do? Spell it out with flowers?

Fitzy was already ushering Lady Susannah away. "Palm-reading is not an exact science," he was saying. "Sometimes one is told things that are *symbolic*, not literally true."

"Symbolic?" the lady said, taking his arm.

"Like in a dream. If you dream of an angry dog, it doesn't actually mean anything to do with a dog . . ."

Lizzie watched, smoldering, as Fitzy led Lady Susannah toward the penny gaffs. He probably thought a visit to the Lobster Boy and the Bearded Woman would take her mind off the scary reading she'd had.

148

"I ain't a liar," Lizzie muttered, clenching her teeth. "And what I saw weren't symbolic, either."

That was what galled her the most. It wasn't Lady Susannah's shock and anger. It was the accusation of lying. If Lady Susannah only knew the trouble Lizzie took to tell people the truth, instead of the comforting lies they wanted to hear . . .

Lizzie marched into her wagon and slammed the door. She thought of Lady Susannah's flushed, angry face. Then she remembered her as she'd appeared in the vision, pleading for mercy. Sobbing, her mouth all twisted in agony . . . it was frightening, all right.

"I've got to help her," Lizzie whispered. "Or she'll end up dead. And I'd never forgive meself." She punched her mattress. "But how can I help someone who just won't listen?"

CHAPTER 15

There were only minutes left until the show was due to start. Lizzie pushed thoughts of Lady Susannah from her mind as she changed out of her clairvoyant's robes. It was a relief to be back in normal clothes. The day had been roasting hot, and the evening ahead was likely to be tropical, too. Sitting in those heavy robes was torture on a day like this.

Lizzie took a shortcut to the show tent, slipping behind the wagons and into a fancy garden. The heat brought the scent out of the exotic flowers and made her feel light-headed and dreamy.

Seemingly out of nowhere, Johnson jumped out from behind a bush. Lizzie screamed as he lifted a shotgun and leveled it at her. "Who goes there?" he barked.

Lizzie gasped for breath and felt her heart pumping. "You scared the life out of me!"

The groundskeeper squinted at her and grunted. "Oh, it's you. The circus girl."

"Who the heck did you think it was going to be? Napoleon Bonaparte?" Lizzie scowled at him as a thought struck her. "You better not be hunting our elephants with that gun. If you so much as touch them, Fitzy will have your hide."

Johnson lowered the shotgun, breaking it open as he did so. "Don't take that tone with me, missy. I'm on guard. That Maharaja might be a trusting fool, but I'm not."

Slowly, it dawned on Lizzie that having the grumpy old man and his gun hiding out here might be a *good* thing. At least he seemed to know Lady Susannah and the Maharaja were in some sort of danger.

"Who exactly are you guarding against?" she asked.

"I don't know yet," Johnson grunted. "But I know this much: if that man's dumb enough to go parading his wealth about through the streets of Whitby, then invite the whole of the town to his castle, he's only got himself to blame if he's robbed again!"

"You think someone's going to try, don't you?"

"God knows there's enough folk here who don't care for him, and they'd love to get their hands on some of the wealth he insists on showin' off." Johnson patted his gun. "Well, I'm not about to let that happen. His money pays my wages."

Lizzie saluted him. "Good. Carry on, man."

Johnson eyed her, unsure if she was making fun of him or not. "On your way," he muttered.

Lizzie ran the rest of the way to the show tent. She felt as if some of the weight had been lifted from her shoulders now that she knew the old curmudgeon was standing watch. He didn't want to see Lady Susannah come to harm any more than she did.

As she neared the red-and-white striped show tent, Lizzie saw all the crowds had already gone inside. Johnson had made her miss the start. Well, never mind — circus people could always go around the back.

Lizzie lifted a canvas flap and slipped into the backstage area with its darkened animal cages and pasteboard scenery standing in wait, then went around toward the back of the audience stalls. She looked past the dividing curtain, saw the seats were packed with people, and grinned to herself. Lady Susannah and the Maharaja were in the very front row, watching the performance. Surely, nobody would try to hurt either of them in front of all these people? There had to be thousands here . . .

Johnson was on guard outside with his shotgun. The show tent was packed. *Nothing bad can happen*, Lizzie told herself. So she settled down to watch for a while.

* * *

Parp! went a horn as Didi, the serious clown, stood stock-still with rice pudding dripping down his face. JoJo threw up his hands in mock horror; the audience roared with laughter. The other clowns bumbled about while Didi chased them from one side of the ring to the other.

Lizzie laughed so hard her sides hurt. So far the show was going perfectly. The people of Whitby were acting like they'd never seen a circus before — and for all she knew, many of them hadn't.

All the hard work her friends had put in at rehearsal was paying off now. The Maharaja had a whole new set of routines to marvel at, and he was every bit as delighted as he had been in Oxford. Lady Susannah just smiled politely, fanning herself, draped in a lace shawl. Lizzie felt a bit sorry for her — she must have too much on her mind to enjoy the fun.

It was sweltering hot inside the show tent. No wonder Lady Susannah had her fan out. The air was growing stuffy, and the smell of so many people packed together — not to mention the circus animals — wasn't exactly pleasant.

Never mind, Lizzie thought. *Only a few more acts to go until the intermission, then we can have cool lemonade with ice from the ice house.*

"Thank you, ladies and gentlemen!" Fitzy called, raising his hands. "Those were, of course, the clowns. And now, a very special treat. Please welcome those daredevil girls, the equestriennes without equal, two matching measures of pure poise and poetry — the astounding Sullivan Sisters!"

Erin and Nora went cantering into the ring and instantly stood up on their saddles, smiling and waving at the audience. Gasps rang out.

Lizzie stared. The twins had told her they were working on new costumes, but they were still wearing the same dresses they'd worn in Oxford. Maybe the new ones hadn't been finished in time. She decided to believe that, and ignore any more sinister explanations that might be creeping into the back of her mind.

Gurinder Bhatti stood up in his seat and applauded. "Go on, girls! *Bravo! Bravissimo!*"

As they passed by, each of the twins gave him a curtsey from horseback. The Maharaja found that charming and blew kisses to them across the sawdust. He didn't seem to notice Lady Susannah slumping lower and lower in her chair.

Lizzie watched closely. The lady fanned herself weakly, but it clearly wasn't doing enough to stop the suffocating heat. Maybe she'd misunderstood the vision of her choking to death? Perhaps this was the moment, and she'd just been gasping for breath? Maybe, as Fitzy had said, the vision was symbolic.

No — there had definitely been a rope round her neck. And now Lady Susannah was whispering something to the Maharaja, who looked sad but nodded and waved her off.

She must be excusing herself, so she can go and get some fresh air, Lizzie realized.

Sure enough, the lady stood and made her way to the main exit. She staggered as she walked and had to steady herself against the backs of the seats. If Lady Susannah left the tent, she'd be exposed to whoever was out there, waiting to do her harm. She had to be warned. But if Lizzie tried to struggle through the audience and catch up, she'd never reach her.

Without thinking twice, Lizzie turned and ran. She sprinted through the backstage area, out through the canvas flap, and around the edge of the show tent, leaping over tent ropes as she went.

Lady Susannah was hurrying across the lawn toward the castle. The fresh air must have perked her up, because she wasn't staggering anymore. Lizzie rushed up to her, shouting as she went: "Your ladyship! Are you all right?"

The lady spun around, saw Lizzie, and let out a startled yelp. She tottered to a halt and pressed her hand to her forehead. "The heat . . . it was too much for me. I am retiring to the castle for a rest."

"You shouldn't be out here on your own! It ain't . . ." Lizzie paused, remembering how angry the lady had been about her violent visions. "It ain't sensible, ma'am, what with your jewelry being stolen and all."

"How kind." Lady Susannah managed a smile. "But you needn't trouble yourself. I promise, I shall lock my bedroom door and check under my bed for criminals."

Lizzie offered her arm. "I'll walk you up there."

Lady Susannah's smile faltered. "That won't be necessary. Now, run along back to your circus. You're missing the show."

"I've seen it before," Lizzie said firmly. She didn't want to miss the final version of Dru's seaside tightrope act — the thought of what might happen if she wasn't there to watch made her squirm — but Lady Susannah's safety was more important.

Lady Susannah heaved a deep, impatient sigh and took Lizzie's arm. "Very well. If you insist on nursemaiding me, I cannot refuse. Not in my weakened condition."

As Lizzie led the lady back to her bedroom, a feeling slowly crept over her. Malachy sometimes read her single-page "penny dreadful" stories bought from the street vendors, and in those, the victims would often report a "feeling of being watched" just before a horrible crime happened. Lizzie knew those stories were just badly written trash. But that was how she felt now, as the lady gripped her arm and they climbed the long avenue of stairs up to her bedroom.

It feels like we're being watched, Lizzie thought.

Lady Susannah's room was high up in one of the towers, but Lizzie insisted on walking all the way up there. When they finally reached the room, Lizzie understood why the lady would feel safe here. It was a wonderful, private haven, hung with medieval-style tapestries and smelling deliciously of lavender and herbs, with a grand high window offering a spectacular view over the gardens. A lamp, turned down low, was burning on the bedside table next to an abandoned copy of a magazine.

Lizzie ran to the window while Lady Susannah settled herself on the bed. "You can see all the way to the sea!" Lizzie exclaimed.

"Yes, you can," the lady said wearily. "Since you're here, would you be a dear and fetch my smelling salts? It's a little brown vial on the dressing table." She closed her eyes and lifted her feet onto the covers, shoes and all.

Lizzie turned to the table with its huge arched mirror and stopped in her tracks. The table's surface was strewn with jewelry — pearl necklaces, silver chains, pendants of ivory and jade — all muddled up as if they were a child's playthings. There, in the middle of the jewels, like an egg in a baby dragon's nest, gleamed the Heart of Durga.

Lizzie forgot to breathe. She was suddenly closer to the giant ruby than she'd ever been before. For a giddy moment, she thought she could feel a mystical heat radiating from it. If she put out her hand, she could touch that beckoning, faceted surface.

She could do more than touch it. She could *take* it. In the mirror, she could see Lady Susannah stretched out on the bed, her eyes closed. It would be a matter of seconds just to snatch up the huge jewel and pocket it.

Well, if this was supposed to be some sort of test, Lizzie wasn't biting. She spotted the little brown bottle of smelling salts, ridged down the side so you could easily feel for it in the dark. She picked it up and brought it over to the bed.

"Here you go, yer ladyship," Lizzie said. "A whiff of these will bring you round."

"Just put them on the bedside table, would you?" the lady murmured. She didn't open her eyes.

Lizzie drew the curtains shut, darkening the room except for the lamp. Just for a moment, she remembered what it had been like to look after her mother, when she'd been slowly wasting away. That was one of many Rat's Castle memories she didn't dwell on often.

"Better put the lamp out," Lizzie said. "Dark and peaceful, that's what you need."

"Leave it lit!" Lady Susannah snapped. "Off you go now, girl. Run along. I need to rest."

"I can sit and keep you company," Lizzie protested. "Just till the show's over, then the Maharaja can come and look after you . . ."

Lady Susannah sat up. "What is the *matter* with you, child?" she said sharply. "Is your head still full of all that nonsense about murder and mayhem? Daggers in the dark, is that it?"

"I know what I saw," Lizzie insisted. "And I know you don't believe it — an' I can't make you — but it's still true! My visions are never wrong!"

"For heaven's sake." The lady didn't conceal her disgust.

Lizzie was so frustrated she felt like shaking her. "It ain't up to me. The stuff I see, it *always* comes true! If I leave you alone, and something happens to you, it's my fault!"

"I don't know whether you're a fantasist or a half-wit, and frankly I don't care," Lady Susannah snapped. "Let me put it to you this way. Either you leave, or I shall have you fired."

"You can't do that."

"Can't I? All I have to do is tell my Maharaja not to pay Mr. Fitzgerald his fee unless you are fired. He will have to get rid of you or face ruin." The lady lay back down on the pillows. "Close the door behind you."

Lizzie's hand shook as she pulled the door shut. She stood in the hallway outside, clenching her fists and breathing hard, refusing to cry, although Lady Susannah's words burned in her stomach. "I'm trying to save your *life*, you stupid woman," she whispered. "One day you'll thank me. Yes, you will. One day."

Lizzie paused at a tower window and looked out across the darkening land. Evening was drawing in. She could see the sea in the distance. There was only one ship still in the bay. Lizzie wondered what it was doing out there, all by itself. Was that a white mist gathering around it?

The next second, her heart missed a beat as a green light shone from the lone ship. *It's the ghost ship — and it's closer to the shore than ever!*

As she watched, the light flickered once, then again. At first, Lizzie thought the lantern was swaying in the wind, but then it suddenly struck her that there was a pattern to it. Three flashes, then a pause, then three more.

She watched the light flicker rhythmically and wondered what it could possibly mean. A ghost with a message from beyond the grave? Or maybe it was something even more sinister than that.

In a sudden flash of certainty that filled her with dread, Lizzie knew her instincts were right. Lady Susannah *was* being watched — and something terrible was going to happen to her. But she couldn't stay here and guard her, not without ruining Fitzy's Circus.

CHAPTER 16

As Lizzie headed back to the show tent, with the moon rising over the distant moors, she heard Ma Sullivan calling her. "Lizzie! Need to borrow you for a minute."

Ma had set up a long row of tables with glasses and teacups borrowed from the castle and the water-boiler borrowed from the tea tent. "Intermission in five minutes," explained Ma Sullivan, "and that group inside is going to want refreshments. I need an extra pair of hands."

Lizzie couldn't very well say no. So she made tea and poured out glasses of lemonade clinking with ice, ready for the crowd, while craning her head around to get a look at the front of the castle, in case some shadowy figure came sneaking up to it.

"Keep your mind on the job, Lizzie," Ma Sullivan scolded her. "Here they come."

Any chance of watching the castle vanished as a horde of excited people burst out of the show tent, chatting among themselves:

"Did you see the way he caught her? Like something out of a pirate adventure . . ."

161

"Daddy, did you see the elephant? Did you, Daddy? Daddy, there were elephants . . ."

"Ooh, that lad, though, the French one . . . he can tightrope into my room anytime!"

Lizzie forced herself to smile and greet people politely. For the next ten minutes, she worked hard serving refreshments and taking money from the grateful Whitby crowd. Eventually, the Maharaja himself came in for a glass of lemonade. He tipped her an extra shilling and stood by the stall chatting with the townspeople.

Lizzie did her best to eavesdrop, but he was just talking about the show. The first half had gone well, by the sound of it. Maybe the locals would warm to him now, as he'd hoped. Although the kind of person who would throw a rock at you wouldn't be likely to change their mind over a night at the circus, would they?

"How's her ladyship?" Lizzie asked when the crowds finally began to ebb. "She looked a bit ill. Someone ought to check on her."

The Maharaja drained his glass. "You're quite right," he agreed. "She'll probably be asleep, and I'll get a flea in my ear for disturbing her, but better safe than sorry, right?"

"Better safe than sorry," Lizzie echoed as the Maharaja headed off.

The gong sounded, calling the audience back inside for the second act. Fitzy stood in the retreating tide of people, looking very proud of himself. He sauntered over to the stall where Ma Sullivan and Lizzie were mopping the sweat from their faces.

"Done all right?"

"You're a sly old devil, Fitzy," Ma Sullivan said. "The Maharaja's holding a free circus, and you go and charge people for drinks on the lawn outside."

Fitzy helped himself to a glass without paying. "I can't very well give 'em away for free, can I? Besides, we're at the seaside. People expect to pay a little extra for their treats. All part of the fun." He frowned. "Speaking of paying, where's our patron?"

"Checking on her ladyship," Lizzie explained. "She felt light-headed and had to go lie down."

Fitzy checked a pocket watch. "Well, we can't start the second act without him. He's the reason we're here."

"There he is!" Lizzie pointed.

"Something's wrong," said Fitzy.

The Maharaja was running. His arms and legs pumped like pistons, and his shirttails flapped behind him. He grabbed hold of Fitzy like a drowning man clutching at a rope. "She's gone!"

"My good man, calm yourself." Fitzy's voice was pure authority. He took the Maharaja by the shoulders and looked right into his eyes. "Tell me what happened."

"Lady Susannah," the Maharaja blurted out, sounding panicked. "She's been kidnapped. Taken from her bed. Everyone warned me about the Whitby curse and the ghost ship, but I dismissed it all as superstition. It's all my fault . . ."

"She couldn't have just gone for a walk? To get some air?" Fitzy inquired.

Gurinder Bhatti shook his head. "Her jewels are gone. There were dozens . . . whoever took her has stolen them, too." His voice rose to a wail. *"The Heart of Durga has been stolen! And my true love abducted!"*

"Oh, no," Lizzie said in horror. "I left her on her own."

"You were the last to see her?"

Lizzie nodded. "I wanted to stay and watch over her — I tried to. But she wouldn't let me. She forced me to leave!"

"So why did you think she needed protecting?" Gurinder Bhatti brandished an accusing finger. "What did you know that you're not telling me?"

A gunshot rang out, echoing across the gardens. The Maharaja jumped. He glanced around, but there was no sign of an attacker.

"It came from over there!" Fitzy said.

"Johnson," Lizzie gasped. "He was guarding the castle with his shotgun. He must have seen someone."

Fitzy set off at a run, and Lizzie and the Maharaja sprinted along behind him. Lizzie had the sinking feeling that they were too late. They'd find Lady Susannah's lifeless body sprawled in Johnson's beloved gardens. Or maybe she'd be found dangling from a tree. That rope around her neck in the vision could have been a noose . . .

They found Johnson holding his gun like a one-man firing squad. One of the barrels was still smoking. He was pointing it at Hari, who was pressed up against a tree, shaking with fear.

"Don't shoot!" shouted Lizzie.

Johnson didn't turn around. "Had to fire into the air to get your attention," he said gruffly. "Tell the Maharaja to get over 'ere. I've caught that boy again."

"I am here," yelled Gurinder Bhatti, "and we do not have time for this!"

Fitzy was livid. "Johnson, what are you playing at? Don't you know what's happened?"

"Huh?"

Lizzie wanted to slap Johnson in his stupid jut-jawed face. "Lady Susannah's been kidnapped, her jewels have been stolen, and you're still persecutin' Hari?"

"He's mixed up in this, whatever's going on!" Johnson insisted. "I saw him sneakin' out of that big tent and scurrying about in the gardens. He'll soon tell what he knows, if you let me beat it out of him."

"That won't be necessary," Fitzy said. He gripped Johnson's arm and forced the shotgun down until it was pointing at the ground. Lizzie hadn't known he was so strong — or so brave. "Hari, explain. Quickly, now. What were you doing out of the show tent?"

"I went to the ice house," Hari stammered.

"Why?"

"The animals were overheating. I thought if I put ice in their drinking water, it would help cool them down. See?" He lifted a bucket full of ice chunks.

"Let the boy go, Johnson," the Maharaja said. "Now, Miss Brown, I beg you, tell me everything you know. My fiancée's life may be in your hands."

Lizzie quickly explained what she'd seen in her visions: the laughing man about to plunge a sword into Lady Susannah, and the hideous image of the lady tied up and begging for mercy. "I tried to warn her, Fitzy," Lizzie finished. "You know I did."

The Maharaja flailed his hands in complete despair. "But who on earth would do this to her? She must have had enemies — someone from her past."

"And she never told you?" Lizzie asked.

"Never. She did not like to speak of her past at all. She said that all that mattered was our future together."

"Gentlemen," declared Fitzy, "we must act immediately. We have to assume her ladyship is still alive, otherwise we would have found her body by now. I expect her abductor is holding her hostage to give himself insurance as he makes his getaway."

"Yes!" Gurinder Bhatti exclaimed, though Johnson looked grim and doubtful. "Saddle up. We will chase them. Johnson, you search to the west, in case they have taken the road toward the moors. Fitzy, come with me on the coast road. The kidnapper may be making for the harbor."

"What about the second half of the circus?" Lizzie said. "It'll have to be canceled!"

"Not a chance," Fitzy answered with a determined look in his eye. "It'll be easier to hunt the villain down if most of the townsfolk are kept here. But the circus does need a ringmaster . . . Hari, take a message for me."

"To Malachy?"

"That's right. I think you know what to say. Gentlemen! To the stables!"

As the three men ran to fetch horses and Hari ran to deliver his message, Lizzie stood alone on the lawn, looking forlornly up at the castle. Somehow, despite her best efforts, some evildoer had crept inside and made off with Lady Susannah.

A cold chill gripped her heart. What had Elsie said about the ghost ship? When it came to harbor, the old legends said, it made off with a living soul. Johnson was local to Whitby. He knew the stories, just like Elsie did. No wonder he'd looked doubtful — he never expected to see Lady Susannah alive again.

Lizzie tried to think. Perhaps the shadowy abductor wasn't someone from Lady Susannah's past, but from the world of the drowned dead? Lizzie thought of the hooded figure standing at the helm of the ghost ship, with two bright gleams in its hood. As she did so, a shivering feeling crawled over her whole body. A vision was coming. A powerful one.

Hari came running back from the show. "Malachy's going to be ringmaster for the second half! He's waited all his life for this . . . wait, what's wrong?"

"Havin' a vision," Lizzie croaked. Like a woman in the throes of a fit, she twisted and shuddered — and found herself staring out to sea.

The crystal-clear vision showed the future. Lady Susannah was alive, but fighting for her life. There were cobwebs in her hair, and her lovely face looked terrified. She was on a small boat, trying to fight off someone Lizzie couldn't see clearly.

Lizzie fell, gasping, to her knees on the soft lawn. "They're headin' to the harbor," she panted. "He's going to take her out to sea on a boat, then kill her."

"Probably planning to dump her body overboard," Hari said darkly. "Where are they now?"

"I dunno. But they aren't on the boat yet, because that vision was definitely in the *future*. So there's still time to stop him!"

CHAPTER 17

"Fitzy and the Maharaja are already riding down the coast road," Hari said. "They'll catch him for sure."

"No, they won't." Lizzie knew it for certain. "Whoever took Lady Susannah hasn't gone down the coast road. I know exactly where they've gone." She ran to her wagon to fetch a lantern, with Hari tagging behind looking confused.

"But the only other road runs toward the moors," he said. "They can't have gone over open ground, surely? They'd be seen!"

Lizzie lit her lantern. "They went *underground*. The old smugglers' tunnel. We learned about it from a local girl the other day."

Hari's mouth fell open. "How do you know?"

"The vision," Lizzie explained. "Lady Susannah had cobwebs in her hair. And how else could they possibly get down to the harbor so quickly without being seen? Come on!"

From inside the show tent, the band struck up an opening fanfare. Lizzie could hear Malachy shouting, sounding clear and confident above the music. He was introducing Mario the Mighty, and the crowd applauded loudly.

Good luck, my friend, Lizzie thought. *You can do this. It's in your blood.*

Lizzie and Hari ran from the warmth and festivity of the castle grounds out into the growing darkness of evening. The wind tasted of rain, and distant thunder trembled across the moors. The weather was hot and humid, and a storm was brewing to blow the lid off it all. From the way the goose bumps rose on Lizzie's arms, she knew it was coming soon.

They ran past the gates and down the road to the waiting clump of trees, which held shadows in among their boughs like thick webs. Lizzie had to use the lantern to find the old brick-lined opening. "Here it is," she told Hari. "The Rum Road."

"Look!" Hari exclaimed. He pointed at a torn scrap of lace from Lady Susannah's shawl, caught on a low-hanging branch. "You were right."

Lizzie led the way down the tunnel, holding the lantern high overhead, while Hari nervously followed. Tree roots had come down through the roof of the tunnel and encircled it like tentacles. In the unsteady light, they seemed to move, as if they were about to stir into life and grab the children.

"Can you smell that?" Hari whispered.

Lizzie could smell lots of things down here — earth, old dead leaves, the damp, musty smell that long-abandoned things have. Then she caught a trace of what Hari was talking about. A bitter, sulfurous smell.

"Gunpowder," she realized. "Malachy smelled it before."

"Maybe someone's planning to blow something up," Hari suggested nervously.

Lizzie shuddered. "It better not be this tunnel. One good sneeze would bring this whole thing down on our heads."

Hurrying down the tunnel wasn't easy. Lizzie knew they were racing against time, but she didn't dare rush. Horrible fates kept arising in her mind. She saw herself stumbling, falling, and smashing the lantern, leaving the two of them trapped in never-ending darkness. Or blundering into a support beam and bringing the ceiling crashing down on them with a roar and a rattle of falling earth.

"How long is this tunnel?" Hari asked in awe, when he realized the exit was still far ahead.

"Half a mile, Malachy reckoned," Lizzie said. She reached a turn she remembered, where Erin had pretended to be an undead smuggler chasing them through the musty dark. It was hard to believe this tunnel had echoed with happy laughter only a day before. Now it felt more haunted than ever.

"It is fascinating," Hari marveled, "to think there is a secret path hidden in plain sight."

Something was nagging Lizzie, and she had to get it off her chest. "I wasn't sure if you were going to come with me," she said.

"Why?" Hari asked. "I'm not frightened of cramped spaces."

"But you don't like the Maharaja much, do you? Yet here you are, helping him get Lady Susannah back. And his jewel, too."

Hari stepped carefully over an ancient shard of wood with a rusty nail in it lying on the tunnel floor. "I don't want Lady Susannah to get hurt," he said quietly. "Keeping her safe is what's important. What I think of Gurinder Bhatti doesn't matter."

When they finally reached the end of the tunnel and opened the door leading into the yard of the Whitby Oyster, silence greeted them. No noise came from the pub, nor from the streets beyond.

The two of them made their way down into the town. All around them, windows were dark, and doors were shut. Traces of mist hovered in the air, and Lizzie glanced in at silent parlors and empty sitting rooms where no fires burned in the grates. It was as if the whole town had been spirited away, its inhabitants turned to wisps of fog that dispersed on the sea breeze.

"They're all watching the circus," Hari said.

"None of them have a clue what's going on," Lizzie agreed. As she listened, she was sure she could hear distant music and cheering carrying on the night air. Then a rumble of thunder drowned it out. The storm was coming closer.

They hurried the short distance down to the harbor, past shuttered shops and shadowed back alleys where anything might be lurking. Boats were moored at the river mouth, but nobody seemed to be on them. Lizzie's chest hurt with the effort of running, and Hari gasped as he ran alongside her.

Finally, they reached the path above the beach. Lizzie collapsed against the railing and looked out over the waves. There, looming out of a bank of mist, was the sinister shape of the ghost ship — a green light shining from its bow, casting an uncanny glow over the water.

Lizzie narrowed her eyes. There was a second light alongside the first. It danced and swayed — a handheld lantern, it could be nothing else.

"He's got her!" Lizzie yelled. "Hari, he's taken her out to the boat!"

"We have to reach them," Hari said. "Maybe I could swim? They aren't too far out yet."

But Lizzie had a better idea. She pointed at Elsie's boat, tied up on the beach. But Elsie was at the circus, with the rest of the town, and they couldn't ask her permission. "We'll just have to borrow it," she said.

Lizzie's legs ached from running, but she forced herself to dash down the stone steps, across the shingle beach, and up to the boat. Together, she and Hari pushed the little rowboat into the foaming surf, wading up to their knees, and climbed in. There was a tangle of netting in the boat's bottom, along with a couple of woven wicker pots.

"Sorry, Elsie," Lizzie whispered as she trod on the net. "Wouldn't be doing this if it weren't life or death!"

Hari took the oars and looked over his shoulder. "That's the famous ghost ship, isn't it?"

"Yes."

He sniffed. "There's that smell again. Gunpowder. And something else, something sharp . . ."

"Never mind that, just row!" Lizzie hollered.

Hari rowed hard. The little boat sloshed away from the beach and quickly closed in on the green light shining from the fog.

The closer they got, the clearer Lizzie could see the ghost ship . . . and in a sudden flash, she realized the fog wasn't fog at all. It was a thick white smoke, and it was pouring from the ghost ship itself.

In that moment, she knew for certain it wasn't a ghost ship, and whoever was at the helm was flesh and blood. The green light, the smoke, the smell of gunpowder . . . everything made sense in the same moment.

"Hari, he's using some sort of *fireworks*! It ain't a real ghost ship at all!" Lizzie exclaimed.

That explains why we smelled gunpowder in the tunnel, she thought. *Someone has been keeping fireworks there. But who?*

A blue blink of lightning lit up the sky. Seconds later, the growl of thunder rolled out across the land and sea. The storm was even closer now. If it caught them on the open sea, the little boat would be helpless.

They had almost caught up with the other vessel now. Lizzie could see the green flare burning and a figure standing behind it, dressed in a hooded robe. The light flashed off a pair of dark glasses.

That explains what I saw, Lizzie thought. *He's wearing dark glasses to protect his eyes from the fireworks. This whole ghost ship was just a hoax . . . a piece of trickery, like a stage effect. But why?*

Whoever was on the "ghost ship" swore when he saw Lizzie's boat drawing closer. The green light suddenly went out, though the swirling fog-like smoke remained. The lantern light vanished a second later.

"Stop where you are!" Lizzie yelled.

The rowboat shuddered as it struck the side of the "ghost ship." Lizzie stood up, the boat wobbling beneath her feet, and peered through the smoke. It was bitter and seared the back of her throat. She could just make out two figures on the deck above, one holding onto the other. She turned up the flame on her own lantern and held it up high. What she saw made her gasp in shock.

"You!?" Lizzie shouted. "I don't believe it!"

Billy, the charming trickster from the beach, stood laughing at her. His hood was drawn back now, and Lizzie could see it was no more than a costume. He had his arms around Lady Susannah.

Lizzie's thoughts rushed back to the day of the circus parade. Poor Lady Susannah had needed Lizzie's help to rescue her from Billy and his oily advances. Clearly, whispering in her ear had only been the start. He was determined to make off with her.

"That's your plan, is it?" Lizzie snarled. "Kidnap the lady, but make everyone think she'd been taken by the ghost ship, so she'd never be seen again?"

"You'd be amazed what the people around here would believe," Billy sneered. "Superstitious bunch of chumps."

"Let her go!" Lizzie yelled.

Billy laughed. "As you wish." He unfolded his arms from around her waist. "Your ladyship, do you want to leave with these children?"

There was a nasty smirk on Billy's face that Lizzie wanted to smack right off. "Come on, quickly," she urged Lady Susannah. "Don't be scared."

Lady Susannah took a hesitant step forward. There was a good three feet of water between the two boats. Lizzie held one of the oars out to her, so she could take it and pull them closer. Lady Susannah grabbed the oar, but to Lizzie's amazement, she tugged it right out of her grip and gave a strange, harsh laugh. As Lizzie stared in surprise, the lady swung the oar like a club.

The paddle caught Lizzie in the face. Blinding pain made her eyes water and her teeth rattle in her skull. "Ow!" she cried, raising her hand to her cheek. Black fireworks were going off in her head. Pain, betrayal, and fear swamped her like a wave. She fought the urge to curl up in a ball.

Lady Susannah yelled at her — and her voice wasn't the fancy, clipped tones of a highborn lady anymore. It was a country accent. "That'll teach you to stop meddling, you little freak!"

As Lizzie staggered back in pain, the taste of blood filling her mouth, a vision rushed into her mind. She was powerless to prevent it. It was as if the blow from the oar had cracked her skull open.

Lady Susannah, in a spangled mask, was lying in a box. Only her head and feet could be seen, poking out of the ends Above her loomed Billy in a magician's costume, his drooping fake moustache held on with glue. He was brandishing a long, curved sword that shone brightly in the strange light from the colored torches burning on the stage.

As the lady screamed theatrically and struggled, Billy raised the sword. "Time to die, my pretty!" he said as he plunged the sword into the box right in the middle section. The audience gasped and applauded. Then he plunged two more swords in. All the while, the lady kept on the screaming.

With a flourish, Billy whipped the swords out and opened the box to reveal Lady Susannah alive and unharmed. They took their bows to a storm of applause. A master of ceremonies came onstage, shook Billy's hand, and called out:

"Ladies and gentlemen, give a big hand for Mister Marvel the Modern Merlin, and his assistant — the beautiful Scheherazade!"

CHAPTER 18

Lizzie couldn't have felt like more of a fool. No wonder Ma Sullivan had thought she'd recognized the lady at the Maharaja's party — she *had*. Billy was the stage magician who'd once called himself Mister Marvel, and Lady Susannah was his assistant . . . his accomplice.

"I got it all wrong," Lizzie gasped to Hari. "Lady Susannah isn't the victim here — she's the culprit!"

"Looks like the secret's finally out," mocked Lady Susannah. Or Scheherazade, or whatever her real name was. "To be honest, I thought you'd figure me out a lot sooner."

"She did," Billy said with a laugh. "See, darlin'? I told you the girl was nothing to worry about."

"Set the sail, Billy. We're leaving." The woman shoved with the oar, pushing the rowboat away and out of reach. "Bye-bye, kiddies!" she said, giving them a mocking little wave.

"Oh, no you don't!" Hari grabbed the fishing net from the bottom of their boat and flung it hard. It opened in flight, falling around Billy.

As the man struggled to free himself, Hari caught the net's trawling rope and pulled it, tightening the net around the magician as if he were a shoal of fish.

Billy laughed, seemingly unconcerned. "Smart move. Did I mention I'm an escape artist?"

"My Mister Marvel can get out of a straitjacket in less than a minute," Lady Susannah mocked. "A fishing net won't pose too much of a problem."

Lizzie glanced back at the shore. Fitzy and the Maharaja would have reached the harbor by now. With any luck, they'd see her lantern's light out at sea and chase them. After all, you could see a lantern all the way from the castle. Lizzie remembered that from when she'd been thrown out of Lady Susannah's bedchamber . . .

Suddenly another piece of the puzzle fitted into place. Lizzie looked inland until she could just make out the castle tower — and a light glowing in Lady Susannah's window.

"No wonder you didn't want me to put the light out!" Lizzie yelled. "It was a signal, wasn't it? And he was signaling back to you from the boat!"

Billy smirked from inside the net. "Clever little scheme, weren't it?" he said. "What with that dopey Maharaja watching her day and night, I couldn't meet up with my Susie for a chat, now could I?"

"I did miss you, my honey bear," cooed Susannah in a soppy voice that made Lizzie want to throw up. She leaned her blond head against his chest. "Of course, I did slip away once in a while . . ."

"I saw you on the beach together!" Lizzie fumed. "Kissing like a pair of lovebirds!"

Billy chuckled. "And that fool thought my beautiful Susie was in love with him. With him! How naive can you get?" He began to wrestle with the net, while Hari struggled to hold him fast.

Lizzie glanced back at the beach again. Lights were approaching on the coast road — the search party! But Billy could sail away at any moment, once he was out of his net. There was only one thing to do. *Billy loves to talk. That's his trademark. If I can just keep him boasting for a while longer . . .*

"There's one thing I don't understand," Lizzie said. "What really happened to the jet necklace?"

Billy tapped his forehead. "You're not very bright, are you? Susie stole it herself, and I sold it!" He wriggled his shoulders, and the net continued to slide off him like a snake shedding its skin.

"So what happens now? You're just going to disappear, are you?" Lizzie yelled.

Billy clapped slowly, mocking her. Lizzie, with a start, realized that he'd gotten his hands out of the net.

"When the ghost ship steals a person away, they're never seen again," Susannah said with a laugh. "Pretty convenient, don't you think?"

Out of the corner of her eye, Lizzie noticed that the search party had boarded a boat and was heading toward them. *I just need a little more time*, she thought. *Play to his vanity, keep him talking.*

"How'd you pick the Maharaja as a target, though?" she asked.

Susannah rolled her eyes. "Good lord. She don't ever shut up, does she?"

"He came to our music-hall show," Billy boasted. "He's a wide-eyed child, that one. When we saw him bouncing around in his seat, we figured he was soft in the head. Ripe for the picking. So me and my sweet Susie decided to take him for all he was worth."

"Your sweet Susie," Lizzie said, practically spitting the words out. "You would have let her marry another man?"

"Oh, they wouldn't have been married long," Billy mocked. "Just long enough for Susie to siphon off every penny of his cash."

"And then, when he was no longer useful?" snarled Hari.

Billy let out an ugly laugh. "He might have vanished without a trace one night. Spirited away by the ghost ship! Never seen again, unless he was washed up on the shore."

"But the famous Lizzie Brown told me we'd never be married," Susannah spat. "I could tell your reading was true. So we went to Plan B."

"What's Plan B?" yelled Lizzie.

With an angry flourish, Billy flung the net away from himself like a cloak. "Getting our hands on this beauty." He dug in his pocket and held up a glittering red object almost as big as his fist. "This ruby's going to make us both rich."

"The Heart of Durga!" Hari gasped. "That's not yours to sell!"

All the struggling with the net had pulled the boats closer together until they were almost bumping. Hari jumped, catching hold of the edge of Billy's boat and heaving himself on board.

"Get out of it!" screeched Susannah. She aimed a vicious kick at Hari's face, but he nimbly dodged out of the way and crouched, glaring at her. She moved between him and Billy, blocking his path to the ruby.

"Give that back," Hari hissed.

"Don't you lay a finger on me," she warned. "I'll show you how dirty a woman can fight."

Hari tried to dash round her, but she grabbed him, ripping his shirt. He shoved her away. As they grappled, Lizzie had a flash of *déjà vu* — she'd seen this in her vision!

In the premonition, Lizzie had thought Susannah was fighting for her life. She was on a small boat, trying to fight off someone Lizzie couldn't see clearly.

But it was Hari! Lizzie had thought Susannah was being murdered. Her vision was coming true, but it wasn't what she'd thought it was at all.

With a yell, Hari gave Susannah a mighty push and sent her sprawling across the deck. Billy staggered backward, still holding the ruby, but now fumbling in his pockets for a knife.

"You ought to be afraid of me, boy!" he shouted.

"Some of his best friends are lions!" shouted Lizzie. "You think he'd be scared of *you*?"

Hari dived at Billy and caught him around the waist in a flying tackle. Billy toppled backward, his arms windmilling wildly. To Lizzie's horror, the ruby flew out of his hand, landed on the deck, and went tumbling across it.

"No!" Hari yelled.

Susannah scrambled after the jewel like a cat chasing a ball of yarn. She was too late. The precious ruby rattled and bounced across the boards like a big glass doorknob, then flew over the side of the boat.

Lizzie didn't pause to think. She moved by sheer instinct alone. She swung her arms and jumped from the boat. Her hands reached out for the jewel.

She snatched it out of the air. It felt so strange in her grasp, heavy and cool as an apple, covered with smooth facets. The next second, she hit the water.

Lizzie was immediately swallowed up by freezing darkness that bit her to the bone. The shock of it almost paralyzed her. Out here, there was no sandy seabed to put her feet down on. The water was deep enough to swallow a tall-masted ship.

But this time Lizzie didn't panic. Despite the intense cold, she knew what she was doing. She dog-paddled hard, clutching the ruby in a fierce grip, until her head broke the water. Puffing and gasping, she swam back toward the boat.

"That's it, Lizzie! Keep going!" It was Hari's voice. She saw him leap from the "ghost ship" back into Elsie's little fishing boat. He held out his hand, and the sight filled her with fresh confidence.

I can do it, Lizzie thought. *Hari knows I can.*

Susannah leaned over the edge of their boat, holding the oar menacingly. "I'm going to smack her one, Bill."

"Wait till she's in the boat, you dumb cow!" Billy raged. "If you put her lights out, she'll drop the ruby!"

"*What* did you call me?" Susannah shrieked.

"You heard!"

"After all I've been through for you?"

"You messed it all up! If you hadn't had a stupid palm-reading off her —"

"PUT YOUR HANDS IN THE AIR!"

The voice booming out across the mist was coming from a large rowboat. Lizzie could see Fitzy, the Maharaja, and a tall, stern-looking man in a black coat. He was holding a pistol. Lizzie took Hari's outstretched hand and gratefully let him haul her onto the boat. Meanwhile, Billy and Susannah slowly lifted their own hands as the police boat approached.

"You two are under arrest," the policeman told Billy and Susannah. Then he turned to Fitzy. "I'm in your debt, gentlemen. We've been after these two for a long time."

"What's the charge?" Billy bellowed.

"Fraud, conspiracy, and robbery for a start," the policeman yelled back.

Fitzy looked satisfied, but the Maharaja just looked heartbroken.

As the boat drew closer, Lizzie was sure she heard the policeman mutter, "And you made me miss the circus, you fool. I had front row seats an' all."

CHAPTER 19

The next morning, instead of leaping out of bed as usual, Lizzie lay dazed and half-awake as the events of the night before rushed back to her. It hadn't been a dream, she knew that. Her hair and the pillow beneath it still smelled of the salty sea.

Once Billy and Susannah had been taken into custody, Fitzy had rowed them back ashore. The Maharaja had draped his silk wrap over Lizzie's wet shoulders, but it hadn't stopped her from shivering all the way. She remembered the terrible look of sorrow on his face.

"I've been a fool," he kept repeating. "Such a stupid, lovesick fool."

Hari, she remembered, had done his best to comfort the Maharaja. "You mustn't blame yourself," the boy had said, sounding more sympathetic than Lizzie would have expected. "She was an actress. A highly talented one. She fooled everybody."

Despite Hari's efforts, the Maharaja's gloom could not be lifted. Not long after everyone had returned to the campsite at Dunsley Castle, and Lizzie was drying off beside the little stove in the tea tent, Fitzy brought word that the Maharaja had left town.

"But where's he gone?" Lizzie had asked.

"He's on his way to London," Fitzy replied. "To Buckingham Palace."

"To see Queen Victoria?"

"Quite so. He may have his ruby back, but the poor fellow has lost the love of his life." Fitzy sighed. "Naturally, the queen knows how that feels. She lost her husband, Albert, not long ago."

It made sense. "I s'pose they can comfort one another, then," Lizzie agreed.

Fitzy patted his pockets. "He has paid us handsomely," he said, "and left orders for our onward journey. This has been most profitable for the circus, and I do hope he manages to also put in a good word for us with the Queen."

Now Lizzie lay under the covers, grateful that she wasn't under the sea at Fiddler's Green. She hoped Elsie could sleep safely now with the knowledge that the ghost ship was nothing but a legend after all. Never again would that misty vessel return to haunt Whitby.

Lizzie yawned, stretched — and suddenly sat bolt upright in bed. "Oh no!" she exclaimed. "I almost forgot what day it is!" She pulled on fresh, dry clothes as quickly as she could, then dug under the bed to retrieve the shell bracelets she'd made for Erin and Nora. There was no paper around to wrap them in, so she put them inside a velvet bag she sometimes used for her tarot cards.

"They'd better not have started their party without me," Lizzie muttered to herself.

The castle lawns were shining with morning dew. All the wagons were quiet and there was no sign of life anywhere. Lizzie was all alone as she ran to the tea tent, bag in hand. She burst in — and every single circus member was there to meet her, smiles on their faces.

"Happy Birthday!" they shouted as one.

"All together now," Fitzy called out. "For she's a jolly good fellow . . ."

Lizzie stood, smiling but bewildered, as the whole circus sang to her. "Which nobody can deny!" they finished. "Hip, hip, hurray!"

"Wait, wait," she interrupted. "You've got it all wrong. It ain't *my* birthday. It's Nora and Erin's birthday."

"I think you'd better ask them about that," Fitzy said, grinning. "Nora? Erin? Explain yourselves!"

The crowd of circus folk parted, as if this moment had been rehearsed — which, Lizzie realized with a shock, it must have been. Because there were Nora and Erin, holding a truly colossal cake, one twin on each side of it.

"It's not right that you've never had a birthday party," Nora said, laughing at the look on Lizzie's face. "And we just couldn't wait until your birthday, which is *months* away yet."

"So you can share our party!" Erin declared. "There are three names on the cake, not just two."

Lizzie didn't know what to say. "I brought you presents," she told them quickly, before sheer happiness made her choke up. "They're, er, both exactly the same, so you needn't fight over 'em."

The cake was escorted off to a side table, while Nora and Erin put the shell bracelets on. "Lizzie, they're beautiful!" Nora said. "You must have taken so much time over them."

"I love mother of pearl," Erin added with a smile. "Goes great with my hair color."

"Girls, we have a confession to make, don't we?" boomed Ma Sullivan.

"Oh, yeah," Nora said. "You see, Lizzie, that time you came into the wagon and we said we were working on new costumes? That was a little white lie."

"We were working on *this*!" Erin said. She produced a hand-sewn bathing suit, striped with black and white, every bit as fine as their own.

Lizzie took it, laughing.

Dru sighed and shook his head. "Does this mean the days of watching Lizzie run into the sea in her clothes are over? I will miss them."

"I'll shove you into the sea in your clothes if you're not careful," Lizzie retorted, and everyone laughed. Her cheeks felt a little hot. All this attention was overwhelming.

"Right," Ma Sullivan said, as if she'd read Lizzie's mind. "It's a glorious morning, and I'm in no mood to sit around inside a stuffy old tent. There's a picnic ready, so let's go to the beach."

Everyone gathered around the huge picnic baskets Ma Sullivan had packed. "Looks like quite a feast, Mrs. S.," Rice Pudding Pete said, "but it must weigh a ton! We're going to need to load up some of the wagons."

"Oh, I don't think that'll be necessary," Fitzy said with a twinkle in his eye. "Hari, Zezete, did you attend to that little matter we spoke of?"

"The elephants are all ready," Hari replied.

So it was that the cast and crew of Fitzy's Circus went trooping through the castle grounds on their way to Whitby beach, with two elephants carrying the picnic baskets. This time, Lizzie got to ride on Akula and admire the splendid gardens from high above.

As they were nearing the great iron gates, Lizzie heard Hari mutter, "Oh, *now* what does he want?"

Johnson, the groundskeeper, was lurking beside the gate with a bucket in his hand. Lizzie braced herself for trouble, though at least he wasn't carrying his shotgun this time. But as they drew closer, she saw he was smiling. Stranger still, he was smiling at Hari.

"I picked these for you," Johnson said, showing Hari the apples that filled the bucket. "From the castle orchards. I reckoned your elephants might like 'em."

"Thanks," Hari said. He looked very confused as he took the bucket. "They love apples."

That's sure taken the wind out of his sails, Lizzie thought to herself.

"I was only trying to look after Dunsley Castle and its master," Johnson said. "But that don't excuse the rough ride I gave you." He hung his head. "I misjudged you, son. You're a brave lad to do what you did." He stuck out his hand awkwardly.

Hari looked at him. For a moment, Lizzie thought he was just going to walk past with his nose in the air and leave the man standing there, looking stupid with his hand out. But Hari smiled, too, and shook Johnson's hand.

* * *

Luckily, despite the sunshine, the beach wasn't too crowded. When the bathers and their families saw the elephants approaching along the coast road, they hurried up to see. The children's admiration turned to wild excitement when Hari led the elephants down the zigzag ramp and onto the beach. Ignoring their parents' warnings, the children flocked around.

While Ma Sullivan busied herself with unpacking the picnic and laying out brightly colored rugs for the circus folk to sit on, Hari gently introduced the crowds of children to Akula and Sashi. Some of the braver children reached up to touch the elephants, then jumped up and down on the spot squealing.

Eventually, some of the parents came and joined them. One hefty fellow with tattooed arms jokingly asked, "How about letting my Bobby have a ride, then?"

"Of course," Hari said, offering his hand. Young Bobby, in a sailor suit, stepped forward with his blue eyes very wide. Hari eased him onto Akula's back, clicked his tongue, and up went the elephant. Bobby clung on, whooping, while the other children danced around, out of their minds with excitement.

"Me next!"

"Can I go on the other one, mister!"

"Dad, Dad, I want one!"

A woman in a shawl sidled up to Lizzie. "It were a lovely circus you all put on," she smiled. "Haven't seen the like in years!"

"You'll come back, won't you?" her husband said. "All of you?"

"I hope so," Lizzie replied, not sure what else to say about the matter.

Once those two had said their piece, the floodgates seemed to open, and soon a crowd of grateful Whitby townsfolk was gathering to say thank you.

"Don't thank us, thank the Maharaja," Hari pointed out. "This whole show was his idea. We wouldn't be here if it weren't for him."

"Well, tell him thanks from me, too," said Elsie, nudging her way through the crowds. "If you hadn't have come, I'd still be frettin' about that ghost ship."

"How did you sleep last night?" Lizzie asked her.

To Lizzie's amazement, Elsie gave her a tight hug. "Like a log, thanks to you. I dreamed I met my brother again. When I woke up, I couldn't remember being so happy."

Fitzy insisted Elsie stay for the picnic lunch. She sat next to Lizzie and the rest of the Penny Gaff Gang. Ma Sullivan passed around plates piled with sandwiches, salad, cold meats, grapes, and bowlfuls of seafood.

"I can't believe that Susannah had the gall to look me in the eye and act like she didn't know me!" Ma Sullivan said, lowering herself to sit beside Lizzie. "I knew I'd seen her before. She and Mister Marvel toured with Kenroy's Circus for a while."

"What was she like back then?" Lizzie asked. She was curious.

"Ah, she was a nasty piece of work," Ma Sullivan said. "All the girls said she thought she was better than everyone else. You've got to admit, though, they pulled off quite a trick."

"*Nearly* pulled it off," said Lizzie quietly, watching the seagulls looping over the waves.

She thought of the palm-reading she'd given Susannah the night of the circus and frowned for a moment. The vision of her future hadn't come true after all. She'd seen Susannah weeping, her arms tied behind her back, pleading not to be killed.

Then the truth dawned on Lizzie. The vision she'd seen had been of Susannah locked up in prison, pleading with her judge to spare her the death penalty for her crimes.

No doubt Billy had been locked up, too. *He might be an escape artist*, Lizzie thought, *but even he won't be able to escape from prison.*

* * *

Fitzy point-blank refused to let anyone do any swimming right after lunch, in case they all got cramps and drowned, so with much protestation the circus children and Elsie were forced to sit and watch others splashing around for half an hour.

Lizzie noticed that Hari kept glancing at Nora as if he was trying to work up the courage to say something. When she got a chance, Lizzie whispered to him, "Spit it out, whatever it is, or we'll be here all day!"

Hari cleared his throat. "Nora?"

"Mmm?"

"I thought you might like . . . that is, you said how much you . . ." Seemingly at a loss for words, Hari held out his hand. A necklace, small but beautifully crafted, dangled from his fingers. Each faceted bead was glittering and black.

"Hari!" Nora exclaimed. "That's not real jet, is it? It can't be!"

"It's real."

Nora took it, handling it gingerly as if it were made of black ice, about to melt away in her hands. "How'd you ever afford this?"

"Just put it on," Hari encouraged her, taking a step back.

Nora shook her head. "Not until you've told me where it came from!"

"I went gathering fossils," Hari explained. "The local jewelers sell them, so they took them in trade. I found some lumps of raw jet, too, and sold them. Eventually, I had enough money for a necklace."

Nora smiled and fastened the necklace around her neck.

That's it! Lizzie thought. *That was the vision I had! I saw Nora putting on the jet necklace, only I thought it might be Lady Susannah's.*

Once again, her visions had all come true. They never failed her.

Erin folded her arms. "So that's why you've been acting so funny, is it? Claiming you had chores to do, then running off to the moors? All along you've been hunting for fossils and jet!"

"I wanted it to be a surprise," Hari said. "Sorry I had to mislead you."

Nora ruffled his black hair. "Ah, we never doubted yeh."

I did, thought Lizzie, guiltily. She smiled, admiring the lovely necklace, but inside she felt terrible. *I doubted all of my friends. I never should have done that. My visions might always come true, but they don't always mean what they seem to mean.*

"You can always trust your own crew," Erin said with a sigh. She looked over to the wall where they'd seen Billy and Susannah sitting that day. "I won't ever trust a performer again, though. They're all flash and dazzle, no substance. All they do is string you along and then break your heart."

"Oh, I don't know," said Malachy. "They're not all bad." He handed her a tiny package.

Erin eagerly unwrapped the gift and revealed a pretty silver thimble with the word "Whitby" engraved in fancy script. She gasped with pleasure as the thimble gleamed in the sunlight. "I can use it when we start working on our new costumes." She winked at Lizzie, adding, "For real, this time."

Erin gave Malachy a quick peck on the cheek, and he beamed brighter than a lighthouse. "Thought you might like a souvenir of our visit to Whitby," he said bashfully. "It's been grand, hasn't it?"

Lizzie nodded in agreement and slowly grinned. *Malachy, you dark horse. You've had a crush on Erin all this time! I always thought you liked one of the twins, and now I know which one . . .*

Dru patted his pockets, searching for something. "While we are giving gifts," he said, "I have *un petit cadeau.*"

"A what?" Lizzie asked.

"A little gift," Dru replied. He passed Lizzie a shining silver comb with a flourish. "Happy non-birthday. Every mermaid needs a pretty comb for her hair."

Lizzie turned away to hide her blushing. "Thanks," she mumbled self-consciously. Suddenly, she felt hot all over and desperately wanted to run into the sea. "I'm going to change into my new bathing suit. My lunch must have gone down by now."

Ma Sullivan laughed. "I'd like to see anyone stop you, girl!"

Moments later, dressed in her new suit, Lizzie went running out to the sea. She plunged in, feeling the cold sea all around her like a mother's embrace, and began to swim with powerful, confident strokes.

I ain't afraid anymore. I can swim! Lizzie thought joyously.

As she came up for air, treading water, she looked back at the harbor and Whitby Abbey overlooking it, high on its cliff, beautiful as a painting. It seemed holy now, not haunted, with sunlight glowing from its ancient walls. Everything was as it should be.

Lizzie smiled, knowing she would remember her first birthday party forever.